© Ceridwen Morris

Sam Lipsyte is the author of a collection of short stories and three novels, including *The Ask* and *Home Land,* which was a *New York Times* Notable Book and received the first annual Believer Book Award. He lives in New York.

Also by Sam Lipsyte

The Ask

Home Land

Venus Drive

The
Subject
Steve

Sam Lipsyte

Picador

Farrar, Straus and Giroux

New York

The
Subject
Steve

A Novel

www.picadorusa.com

Picador® is a U.S. registered trademark and is used by Farrar, Straus and Giroux under license from Pan Books Limited.

For information on Picador Reading Group Guides, please contact Picador. E-mail: readinggroupguides@picadorusa.com

Design by Dana Leigh Treglia

Picador ISBN 978-0-312-42997-3

First published in the United States by Broadway Books, a division of Random House, Inc.

First Picador Edition: March 2011

10 9 8 7 6 5 4 3 2 1

For Ceridwen

Items #1

Bastards said they had some good news and some bad news.

"Stop," I said. "I've heard this joke before."

"What joke," said one of them, the Mechanic.

"He means that joke," said the other, the Philosopher. "That bit about the doctors. He thinks we're doctors."

"Aren't you?" I said.

They had white coats, their own wing.

"This ain't no joke, Jack," said the Mechanic.

My name's not Jack.

My name's not Steve, either, but we'll get to that.

"We have some good news and some bad news."

I can't remember what the good news was.

The bad news was bad. I was dying of something nobody had ever died of before. I was dying of something absolutely, fantastically new. Strangely enough, I was in fine fettle. My heart was strong and my lungs were clean. My vitals were vital. Nothing was enveloping me or eating away at me or brandishing itself towards some violence in my brain. There weren't any blocks or clots or seeps or leaks. My levels were good. My counts were good. All my numbers said my number wasn't up.

Fine fettle for a dead man, they said. Days, they said, months, maybe a year, maybe more than a year. It was difficult to calculate. Nobody had ever died of this before. By their calculations there could be no calculations.

"You'll have to live like the rest of us," the Philosopher told me. "Just less so."

"You mean more so," I said.

"No time for semantics," said the Mechanic. "You'd best get ready."

I readied myself for the period in which I'd have to get ready. I waited for the time during which I'd have to wait. I tied up loose ends, tidied up accounts, put my papers in order, called old friends. I didn't really have any papers.

I did have friends.

I had Cudahy.

I called Cudahy.

"I'm coming to see you," said Cudahy.

"Come soon," I said.

I called my ex-wife, nothing if not a loose end, or at least a bit of untidiness, what with all we had left unaccounted for.

"I knew you'd call," said Maryse. "I had a dream about you last week. You were walking through the pet food aisle at the supermarket and a kind of viscid bile was streaming down your chin."

"It wasn't a dream," I said. "I'm dying."

"I know, baby. I'm dying, too. But we've tried so many times already. We just have to learn to live with things the way things are. Things are not so bad. Truth be told, I'm not unfulfilled by William."

"William's a very good fellow," I said.

"He's not you," said my ex-wife, "but then again, you're not him."

William had once been my hero. Then he whisked away my wife. Now he was a very good fellow, a fucker, a thief. He deserved to die of whatever everybody had ever died of before, but with more agony, a heavier soiling of sheets.

"You may not hear from me again," I said.

"That's probably a wise choice," said Maryse.

"I don't think it's a choice," I said. "I'm really dying."

"Don't threaten me," said Maryse.

I quit my job, jammed a letter under my supervisor's door. He waved me in anyway. It appeared I had to interview for the right to quit.

"What kind of contribution do you feel you've made to the agency?" said my supervisor.

"I was quiet in my cube," I said. "I never fastened personal items with tape to the wall. I leered at female coworkers in the most unobtrusive manner possible. My work, albeit inane, jibed with the greater inanities required of us to maintain the fictions of our industry. I never stinted on pastries for my team."

"What makes you think you're qualified to relinquish your present position?"

"All of the above," I said. "Plus the fact that I'm dying."

"Dying of what?" said my supervisor.

"It's new," I said.

Home, I threw away my watches, my clocks, my clock-radios. I kept my Jews of Jazz calendar up on the kitchen door. The knowledge of days was crucial, I decided, the marking of hours a mistake. I spread old photographs out on the coffee table, Scotch-taped a nice lifetime of say-cheese to the walls. Tacky, maybe, a mural like this, but what's tacky to the terminal? I studied the faces of all those friends and family and friends of the family. There they posed, on throw rugs, on sofas, in fields. Sitting or standing. Alone, in groups, in tandems, foregrounding fountains, friezes, pagodas, squares. Some of them were still living, others still dead. They had lived known lives, died, well, understandably. What I was dying of, I mused, nobody anywhere had a picture of somebody dead from it.

I mused this for a damn long while.

I mused this for almost a day.

I called up my daughter at the School for Disaffected Daughters. My ex-wife and I had agreed it was the best place for our Fiona to flourish and grow. We'd married out of school, Maryse and I, maybe just to be rebellious, fallen into faction-hood the way rebels at rest will do. The worse things got, the more we cooed our devotion. Maybe our devotion was a blister we were waiting for the proper time to pop. I guess we wanted to see the pus.

"Fiona," I said, "I have some news."

"Don't tell me," she said.

"I have to tell you."

"Tell me later," she said. "I've got a lot on my plate."

"I'm going to tell you now."

I told my daughter I was dying of something no one had ever died of before.

"A rare disease?" she said. "Wow, that's wild."

"Not rare, Fiona. Mysterious. Rare would imply other sufferers. I'm the only one. Or at least the first. The pioneer. Think mud barns and locusts, rough cotton bonnets."

"I don't follow," said Fiona. "Do you feel sick? Is it some kind of therapeutic bonnet?"

"I feel fine," I said. "I'm in fine fettle for a dead man, in fact."

"Is that from a song?" said Fiona.

"Maybe it will be," I said. "Maybe I'll write a song."

"I've got to go," said Fiona. "I'll check in to see how you're doing."

"You mean to see if I'm dead."

I'd been a bad man. Bad hubby. Bad dad. Well, not bad. Less than bad, which was worse. But I'd paid for it. I mean, I was paying for it.

"Please, Daddy, don't say that," said Fiona. "What if this is the last time we speak?"

She hung up on me, on "speak." Typical of her disaffection. Typical of her disbelief. I figured she figured it all for a song or a game. What else is it when you're thirteen and test just shy of genius? When she has to pick the suit they bury me in, then she'll believe it. When she has to pick the urn they pour my burnt bones in.

Weekdays were clinic days. The Philosopher and the Mechanic wished to meet with me often as I was such a special case. Already my malady had begun to further their careers. They were collaborating on a book based loosely on my autopsy.

"You look amazing," said the Mechanic. "Doesn't he look amazing?"

"Luminous," said the Philosopher. "Luminous with this mysterious rot."

We sat on overstuffed sofas in the Special Cases Lounge. A man in black surgical scrubs brought us tea and lemon cake.

"Can I get a drink around here?"

"Not officially," said the Philosopher, "but here."

He plucked a bronze flask from his coat.

"Brandy?" I said, sniffing it.

"Cognac," said the Philosopher. "With a dash of methamphetamine."

"Tell us," said the Mechanic, "how are you coping with the emotional devastation of your predicament? How do you go on living knowing you are going to die?"

"How do you?" I said.

Both men nodded, made noises in their mouths, scribbled on the notepads in their laps.

"What?" I said. "What are you doing?"

"I don't know what he's doing," said the Philosopher. "I'm just jotting down some top-secret notes."

They were both bastards, but at certain moments I got the feeling the Philosopher was also a prick.

"Did you run those tests yet?" I said.

"Which tests would those be?" said the Mechanic.

"The ones you said you were going to run to get a better idea of how much time I had left."

"*Have* left," said the Mechanic. "You're not dead yet."

"Excuse me?" I said.

"Fascinating," said the Philosopher.

"We conducted the tests," said the Mechanic. "Frankly, they left us more baffled than before. Honestly, I can't tell you anything more than we've already told you. You're dying. You're dying quite quickly. The rest is a mystery better explored in our upcoming book."

"Your book," I said. "I don't give a rat's ass about your book. What about the cure?"

"Cure for what?" said the Mechanic.

"You know damn well it doesn't have a name," I said. "You're the ones who didn't name it."

"You see our problem," said the Philosopher. "Who's going to grant us the time, the money, the facilities to research a cure for a nameless ailment from which one person presently suffers? What are we going to do, mount gala events to raise funds for the Fight to Save Steve from Whatchamacallit? By the way, how's the hooch? The speed gives it a nice bite, right?"

"My name's not Steve."

"No, but my point stands."

"We need more clients," said the Mechanic. "Or patients, if you prefer. Until then, I don't know what to tell you. We'll do what we can."

"What's in our powers."

"Our purview."

"Our ken."

My daughter disaffected, my ex-wife whisked, me dying quite quickly of radically accelerated Whatchamacallit, I decided, here in the grips of aimless urgency, to sin.

By sin, I mean fun, harmless.

I got a deal on some pharmaceutical-grade cocaine from the Philosopher. The Mechanic gave me a phone number, instructed me to ask for either Greta or Clarice.

I got Greta.

Greta brought Clarice.

Both of them were tall and bony with bone-colored and ash-colored hair.

Both of them were professionally, abnormally delicious.

"Kiss the dead man!" I said, throwing off my robe. "Fondle his fettle!"

We passed some days this way, prancing, sucking, snorting, heaving, shrieking. We ordered in dinner, Indian, Chinese. Greta, an aspiring dramaturge, directed us in choice bits of Aristophanes. Clarice hand-tinted my knees for a ritual dance of our own device. We built cities with popsicle sticks, baked peanut brittle, fudge. We invented a game whereby each woman pissed down my throat and I, blindfolded, guessed by odor alone whose water it was.

Easy, what with Greta's penchant for wheatgrass juice.

When the sun rose on the last day Clarice shook me awake.

"Time to settle up," she said.

I figured it was money well spent. What's seventy-three thousand dollars to a guy with Whatchamacallit?

I sat there the rest of the morning wondering how to tell Fiona she was now officially a hardship case.

Then someone was knocking the knocker on my door.

"You'll feel better once they come up with a name for it," said Cudahy.

He stood in my kitchen and stirred his tea, an enormous man in a neon-flecked track suit.

He'd once captained the national shot-put team.

"I don't give a damn about the name," I said. "I just want to live."

"I want you to live, too, buddy," said Cudahy. "Believe me."

"I do believe you," I said.

Cudahy was my best and oldest friend. Best and boon. Maybe we'd drifted apart at times, I into the smoked-glass murk of corporate life, Cudahy into his far-flung entrepreneurial endeavors, which included a stint in foreign bride importation, but we'd never let the thread of our friendship snap. There was too much truth and not enough language between us for that.

We'd run the beet fields and subdivision lots of our boyhood together, slept under the yard stars, stolen off with the family whiskey into the wooded night. We'd scorched town birches with our homemade flamethrowers, burned out all the gypsy moth cocoons. Moth-O-Caust, we'd called it. We'd stood behind the toolshed and listened, amid the clatter of rake tines and paint tins, to our fathers make shuddering men of each other.

This last we'd never discussed.

"You know," said Cudahy now, "you should have called me

after Maryse left. I could have gotten you a new missus for less than ten grand. Tits, an adorable accent. Grateful to be free of the emerging-market yoke."

"What's done is done," I said.

"That's the attitude," said Cudahy. "That's the attitude of a man who wants to live!"

"Don't saw the pine for me yet," I said.

"That's it, baby!" said Cudahy. "No pine, no crepe, no wreaths!"

He spun a hard orbit on the linoleum. Tea ribboned out of his cup. The cup shattered on the wall.

"Shit," said Cudahy.

"Nice put," I said.

Cudahy took the spare room, kicked in expenses from the fat roll in his track suit pocket. We cooked lavish meals from newspaper recipes—veal marsala, rack of lamb—played black-jack past midnight, watched old westerns on the VCR.

Every time there was shoot-out Cudahy would recount his own days of gunplay, usually some kind of pimp jump in the lime-colored corridors of a formerly Socialist apartment block.

"They got my driver Vlad in the head, point-blank," he said one night. "I figured I was a goner until I stumbled across a ventilation duct. Hard to believe I fit, but I did. And so here I am. And here you are. Death's luck goes south, too, you know. Hit me."

"I think the reaper's due for a run."

"Don't talk that way," said Cudahy. "This living and dying shit, it's all a matter of attitude. It's like you're at the Worlds with a couple of fouls and you need one clean put to qualify.

The Swedish judge is gunning for you and you're thinking, 'I will stay in the circle, there is nothing for me outside the circle. Fuck Scandinavia.' "

"What are you talking about?"

"Say it: There's nothing for me outside the circle. Fuck Scandinavia."

"There's nothing for me outside the circle. Fuck Scandinavia."

"Exactly," said Cudahy. "Worked for me. I silvered. Then I got out of the shot-put racket for good. I mean, chucking a steel ball over and over again. For what? The travel, sure, but all in all it was a waste of time. And you know what else? When you're a great shot-putter, they hate you for it. They really do. Not true of, say, the discus. The discus-throwers have a feeling of community. They have that statue. Hit me. Fuck, busted."

When I phoned the clinic to confirm my next appointment, the Mechanic took the call himself.

"We've got some exciting news," he said. "A breakthrough. I can't tell you over the phone, though."

Cudahy popped a bottle of raisin schnapps.

"To beginnings, breakthroughs, fresh starts," he said. "May the upshot of all this be nothing more than a beautiful new-found invigoration that informs your long years ahead."

"That's nice," I said.

"It's an old peasant saying," said Cudahy. "The literal translation is 'Better you fuck yourself than they fuck you.' Good luck tomorrow. I'll be waiting with some coq au vin."

. . .

The next day the nurse led me past the Special Cases Lounge and through a slim metallic door. We stepped into a bright amphitheater, a room like a grooved well. The Philosopher and the Mechanic stood down at the bottom of it behind a semitranslucent scrim. Dozens of others filled the raked seats. Some craned back to catch my eye, nod, enact hopeful semaphore with their thumbs. The Philosopher stepped out from behind the scrim. A lectern rose into his hands from some hushed hydraulics in the floor.

"Good morning," he said. "Shall we begin? Now as some of you from the press may be unfamiliar with medical jargon, I'll try to stick to layman's terms. But first, a small caveat. While our tests can't be considered foolproof, the sheer quantity of data and the unequivocal agreement of it cannot be wished away. Since we have nothing comparable by which to judge the subject's condition, there is, to be quite candid, some element of faith involved, but I would by no means refer to it as a *leap* of faith. Consider it more on the order of a small hop. Or perhaps even a skip. Okay, then, on to the main presentation of our body, or rather, well, you know what I mean . . ."

There were giggles in the gallery. The lights dimmed. The Mechanic slid a videocassette into a dark notch in the wall. Out of speakers mounted in the ceiling came the whir and sputter of an old film projector. Nice touch, I thought, listened as a chimey melody, familiar somehow, seeped into the room. It was American educational music, that old warped hope in major chords, and it bounced along to the vistas skating by on the screen: mountains and mountain valleys, jungles and jungle clears, lakes, rivers, streams, each yielding to the next in a bright ceremony of splice and dissolve.

Last was a light-filled forest, where all manner of creature began to stir, make their first nervous pokes from burrow and mound. I'd seen footage like this before, felt fourteen again, dozing in my snowboots, waiting for the afternoon bell. How much I'd always envied the tight life of voles. The hidey hole was happiness.

No expectations down there.

Now the shot pulled out a bit. Here a stunted horse drank from a creek. There an odd bird jerked worms from the earth. Here came a rustle in the brush, a gentle tremoring that sent bugs the size of bullets to wing. Something huge burst into view, a shambling immensity I knew from coloring books, dioramas of yore. The woolly mammoth. Hairy-hided. Shovel-tusked. A great shaggy thingness. It looked about with what could have been innocence and not a little fear in its eyes. I wondered how much it cost to rent a toothless elephant, trick him out for another geological age. There wasn't much time to wonder. The music tripped into a darker key, some molester-on-the-carousel lilt. It was the end of innocence, or the end of something.

It was bum luck for the mammoth.

A band of humanoids lumbered up, a hunting party, crude men with crude spears in their tufted fists, loud language on their tongues. They whooped and hollered, circled the beast, rushed in and out and in again, stabbed until the mammoth's hide blew bright spouts of mammalian blood. The woolly fellow thumped to his knees, bellowing, bellowing, us thrust up now into the black pain of his mouth. His cries and the taunts of the hunters started to fade. There was darkness now, silence. There was darkness with a few faraway pricks of light. The universe. Universal shorthand for the universe.

We were moving through it now. We were gliding toward

a greenish-bluish ball. Our ball, the home sphere. Sea and tree and all those organic shenanigans, all that fluke life. We were flying right smack into the middle of the fucker, flying and flying until it wasn't flying anymore, it was falling, and we were falling now through clouds and sky and down upon the body of a city, row house bones and market hearts and veins of neighborhood, arterial concretions of highway and boulevard and side street, falling now to a low float over pavement, a hover here in some lost alleyway, a superannuated little gland of a place, where a solitary figure walked with his hands stuck in his windbreaker. The figure began to glow, as though suddenly sensor-read, his organs swirls of grained color, his skull a glassy orb of dim pulses and firings, the lonely weak electrics of homo erectus. The man stooped for his shoelace. The picture froze at the beginnings of a bow knot. Through the speakers came the sound of sprocket jump, the flutter of reel's end. The screen swiped to test bars. The music leaked away. The lights went up.

The Mechanic took the lectern, spoke into a thimble he'd slipped upon his thumb.

"Any questions?"

There were questions.

"Should we assume the figure, the visible man, as it were, is the subject?" called a woman with a series of laminated cards clipped to her pantsuit.

"What's with the woolly mammoth?" said a kid with a video rig strapped parrot-like to his shoulder.

"Forget that," said an old man in a hunting vest. "What is the point of any of this? Is this some kind of gag?"

"I assure you," said the Philosopher, leaning into the Mechanic's amplified thumb, "this is no gag. Nor could it be construed as a bit. The visual aid is merely meant as a tool to help you better understand the scope of what we're about to tell you. Ladies and gentleman, the subject, who, as some of you may already have ascertained, is seated here among us, which I note as a precaution against insensitive comments regarding his condition, this subject is the first known sufferer of what I believe will and should be referred to from now on as Goldfarb-Blackstone Preparatory Extinction Syndrome, named, I might add, for its discoverers, Dr. Blackstone and myself."

"Without being technical," said the kid with the parrot cam, "what exactly is the nature of PREXIS? PREXIS for short, right? I mean, what's the deal, nontechnically speaking? And why should we care, given all the diseases out there right now?"

"To put it bluntly," said the Mechanic, "those other diseases already have a name. And with it, a cause: viral infection, chemical compromise, cellular glitch, inheritance on the genetic level. This syndrome, though now named, still has no identifiable cause, which does not mitigate its unquestionable fatality. This man is going to die. But here's the kicker: he's going to die for no known reason. Maybe not today, maybe not tomorrow, but eventually, and irrevocably. He may show no signs of it yet, but he will, trust me. And though he may be the first, I assure you he is not alone. Like the beast in the film, and the prototypical bipeds who felled it, all of us here, too, will someday be extinct. And not from nuclear catastrophe or chemical weaponry or environmental collapse, but from something else entirely. Who knows? Perhaps the cause is sheer purposelessness. At any rate, be advised, this subject, Steve, this mild-mannered thirty-seven-year-old ad man, is but the first in line. Maybe you've been lucky enough to dodge everything else, the cancers, the coronaries, the aneurysms, but do not consider yourself blessed. Goldfarb-Blackstone, or PREXIS, if you will, is guaranteed to claim us all."

"Aren't you just talking about death?" said the old man.

"Unfortunately, yes," said the Mechanic.

"But don't we already know about death?"

"What do we know? We know nothing. Now at least perhaps we have what little light the work of Dr. Goldfarb and myself can shed on it."

"I'm interested in what you mean by purposelessness," said the woman in the pantsuit. "Do you mean boredom? Do you mean to say this man is actually going to die of boredom?"

"That's one way of putting it, yes," said the Philosopher.

"Dynamite," said the woman, darted out of the room.

"Why didn't you tell me sooner?" I said, back in the Special Cases Lounge.

"We weren't sure."

"We couldn't be certain."

"All the data accounted for."

"All the numbers in."

"Sorted."

"Crunched."

"Mashed."

"Mealed."

"Until a granular quality obtained."

"Then checked and counterchecked against findings in our database."

"Adjusted for error."

"Baseline error."

"Human and otherwise."

"Human and counterhuman."

"We had to be precision-oriented on this one. Or orientated."

"Either way."

"We had to be scientists about it."

"If we're not scientists, what are we?"

"If we're something else, who are the scientists?"

"So," I said, "how long have I got?"

Cudahy was waiting on the corner near my building. It looked like there'd been some sort of accident. News trucks and radio cars cordoned off the better part of the block. Cudahy threw a parka over my head, guided me up a hillock of root-ruptured pavement toward my door.

"Don't answer the vultures," said Cudahy.

"Which vultures?" I said.

Here they were upon us, pressing, pecking through my fuzzy sheath.

"How does it feel to be dying?"

"Do you believe you are bored to death?"

"Have you had any further contact with the mammoth?"

Cudahy shouted them all down. I felt his huge arms wrap around my head.

"Scum," said Cudahy, bolted the door behind us. "Wish to God I had Vlad with me. That guy sure knew what to do to a journalist."

I let the parka slip to the floor.

"What's happening to me?" I said.

"Hell if I know," said Cudahy. "Why can't they let a man die in peace?"

"I'm in fine fettle," I said.

"Sure you are."

"All I did was go in for a checkup."

"That's how they get you," said Cudahy.

He cracked a bottle of beef-flavored vodka, turned on the TV. The woman in the pantsuit beamed up from my stoop. She fiddled with a coil of metal in her ear.

"Yes, Mike," she said, "he appears to be barricaded in this building you see behind me. And, truthfully, I can't say I blame him. Who wants to be the pace car in the race to oblivion? But there's another question, Mike, which I think you broached, or maybe breached, earlier. How do we know he's the only person on the planet with Goldfarb-Blackstone, or PREXIS, as it's so rapidly come to be known? It's hard to believe that this man, this so-called Subject Steve, is even the only victim of terminal ennui in this city. And if there are others, are they dying, too? Are we all, perhaps, dying? Have we, perhaps, always been dying? It's too early to tell."

"This is insane," said Cudahy. "A mass hallucination. I've read about this kind of thing. You do a lot of reading on the track and field circuit. Downtime. Cafés. You get educated. History is full of this phenomenon. It'll blow over."

"I don't see it blowing over," I said.

"It's just started to blow, buddy. There's a whole blowing-over process. Anyway, you've got more important things to think about. You're still, on a personal level, dying."

"But I'm in fine fettle," I said.

"Fettle is irrelevant," said Cudahy. "Science has proven that much."

Now a man I knew appeared on the screen. He sat at an office workstation, his thin hair blending with the fabric of the cube-wall weave.

"One thing I can tell you about the subject," said the man, "he always bought doughnuts for his team."

"Pastries!" I said. "Better than doughnuts!"

"It's okay," said Cudahy. "Calm down."

"It wasn't doughnuts."

"It's okay," said Cudahy.

"What are they talking about, boredom?" I said. "I've never been bored. Lonely, tired, depressed, of course. But not bored."

"I think they mean that as a euphemism," said Cudahy.

"A euphemism for what?"

"I'm not sure I follow," said Cudahy.

This was about the time I started to weep. This was the kind of weeping where after a while you're not quite sure it's you who's still weeping anymore. Some wet, heaving force evicts your other selves. You're just the buck and twitch, the tears. You fetal up and your thoughts are blows. Phrases drift through you. Rain of blows. Steady rain of blows. There's no relent. There's no relief. The hand of a comforting Cudahy is a hunk of hot slag. The world is a slit through one bent strip of window blind. The noise of the city, the hum of the house, the hiss of the television, is wind.

I fell asleep, woke to a bowl rim at my lips.

Fiona.

Dimly, men in Stetsons rode past boomtown facades and out onto a pixilated plain.

"I love this part," I heard Cudahy say, dimly.

"Fennel soup," said Fiona. "Drink."

"They're doomed," said Cudahy. "They know they're doomed, and they also know their only shot at grace is precisely in that knowledge. There's an army of vicious Mexicans out there waiting to shoot them to pieces."

"I'd like to see the Mexican side of the story," said Fiona. "I'd like to read an oral history from the Mexican perspective."

"An oral history," said Cudahy. "I bet you would, honey."

"Gross."

"What's going on?" I said. I figured they needed a chance to adjust, to my state, to their consideration of my state. My worry was that I could sleep too much. A dying man sleeps too much, maybe his power slips away.

I needed all the power in my purview, my ken.

Cudahy muted the doomed hooves.

"Daddy," said Fiona.

"So," I said, "you heard. You came."

"PRAXIS," said Cudahy.

"PREXIS," said Fiona.

"You didn't seem so worried before," I said.

"I didn't know how serious it was."

"Baby, I have some bad news. About your educational opportunities."

"It's okay. Uncle Cud told me. I hope the fucking was worth it."

"Only time it's not worth it is when it's free," said Cudahy.

"Daddy, I want you to know I'm going to be here for you. That part is settled. Don't argue with me. It's what I need to do now. For me as much as for you."

"Thank you, baby," I said, and sang to her, weakly, the song about aardvarks I had sung to her in the days before her disaffection.

Then I spit up some fennel shreds.

The next morning Cudahy went out for food, the early papers. I watched him pilot his bulk down the stoop, disappear behind a satellite truck. My good Cudahy, back from the wide strange world.

My fondest Fiona.

"You'll ruin the paint with all this tape," she said, pulling my scrapbook mural down.

I thought back to the time Fiona was six, seven, caught a double zap of chicken pox and scarlet fever. She got so quiet there on the living room carpet playing divorce with her Barbies. The sores spread and her blood boiled. We watched her body take on the silken deadness of her injection-molded friends. It all came to high drama, or my high dramatics, me running crazy through the neighborhood with my doll-daughter in my arms, Maryse screaming for me to come back.

"I've got us a cab, schmuck!"

The doctors shamed us for our delay. Maryse and I, we'd been inches from the abyss of nefarious parentage, practically Christian Scientists, but Fiona would live. It must have been our luck that got us so hot, basted us both in visions of hump and dazzle. Or maybe it was some awful need to screw within wad's shot of the abyss. Home, we drank a little wine, put on some of that sticky saxophone music we used to keep around to drown out the bitter squeaks in our hearts. We gripped each other's privates and started to kiss, but our mouths were pruned things, insipid divots. My wife's wetness was all for

William the Fulfiller now. We conked out drunk on the carpet, woke up around dinnertime, checked in on our baby. Fiona was bent up in her fever's waning. Maryse and I held hands beside the little plaid bed.

"I'm leaving you," said my wife.

"I know," I said.

Fiona claimed she remembered none of it, but she still bore a mark from those days, a pock where a scab must have flaked, smack between her dry green eyes.

It was about the size of a sunflower seed.

Cudahy came back with cabin food. Siege supplies. Soup cans and sandwich meats and bouillon cubes in silver foil. He pulled a newspaper from the grocery sack, folded to an item: "Doc's Prog for Our Kind: Game Over." Beneath my ex-wife's picture was a caption: "Ex-Hubby the New T. Rex."

"Where'd they get the photo?" I said.

"Eye in the sky, probably," said Cudahy. "Or the DMV."

"Mom gave it to them," said Fiona. "She left a message on my cell. She's getting calls from talk shows. She wants to know how you feel about her speaking publicly on the matter."

"You mean whoring herself."

"Sharing her experience, hope, and strength."

"Tell her she can do whatever the hell she wants."

"I knew you'd say that so I already said that."

"There's a guy out there," said Cudahy. "He's offering his help."

"Reporter?" said Fiona.

"Don't think so," said Cudahy. "He told me to give you this."

It was a mimeographed brochure, lettered in splotchy monastic script.

Have you been left for dead?
Do you number among the Infortunate—
shrugged off by family, friends, physicians, priests?
Have you been told you're beyond all hope?
Are you incorrigible, inoperable, degenerative,
degenerate, terminal, chronic, and/or doomed?
Are you lost, are you crazy, or just plain sick?
Maybe you should snuff it, friend.
Go ahead.
Pull the Trigger.
Turn up the Gas.
Do it.
Do it, coward.
Did you do it?
You didn't, did you?
Okay, don't do it.
You're not worth the
mess you'll make. Not yet.
Here's a better idea:
Call the Center for Nondenom-
inational Recovery and Redemption and deliver
back unto yourself your dying body and your dead
soul.
No malady, real or imagined, is too difficult to
cure.
Forget the scientific phonies and the quacks of
holistic boutiques.
Forget the false love of New Age shamans.
Forget the false touch of healing retreats.
Your health, your freedom, your salvation is a
toll-free call away.

Ask for Heinrich.
All major credit cards accepted.

Squeezed along the margin in fountain ink was this: "I Have the Cure. —H."

I made of this inanity a nice coaster for my coffee mug.

"They'll really be coming out of the woodwork now," I said.

"What woodwork?" said Cudahy. "We're on an island of concrete."

Items #2

Walking back to the clinic for my next appointment a few weeks later, I saw what Cudahy had meant. I'd lived in this city long enough to forget the absurdity of the place, all these surfaces refracting us in shatters, this tonnage that bore down on us with hysterical weight.

Someday sectors of this city would make the most astonishing ruins. No pyramid or sacrificial ziggurat would compare to these insurance towers, convention domes. Unnerved, of course, or stoned enough, you always could see it, tomorrow's ruins today, carcasses of steel teetered in a halt of death, half globes of granite buried like worlds under shards of street.

Sometimes I pictured myself a futuristic sifter, some odd being bred for sexlessness, helmed in pulsing Lucite, stooping to examine an elevator panel, a perfectly preserved boutonnière.

I'd be the finder of something.

Now, walking along, I had only the sense of losing myself.

Yes, I could perambulate unpestered, unthronged. My saga was stale. There were fresh griefs upon us. A beloved lip-sync diva had choked to death on a sea bass bone. The troops of our republic were poised on the border of a lawless fiefdom in Delaware. The Secretary of Agriculture had been exposed as a fervent collector of barnyard porn. Worse, he had a yen for the young ones, the piglets, the foals. Bestiality was one thing, opined the ethics community, but for God's sake, these were babies. There were wars and rumors of war and leaks of covert ops. There were earthquakes, famines, droughts, floods. A certain movie star had made box office magic once more.

The *National Journal of Medicine*'s scathing rebuke of the veracity of Goldfarb-Blackstone Syndrome, its excoriation of the ailment's namesakes as "freakshow impresarios," had barely made the back pages, the spot after the break.

The air was out and I was glad of it. My fine fettle continued to obtain. Still, I somehow felt bound to these men, Goldfarb and Blackstone, the Philosopher and the Mechanic. They'd shocked me into keener living. I was brimming with bad poetry and never reading the financials. I can't say I knew what counted in life but I was beginning to glimpse what didn't. I had Fiona back, and Cudahy, too.

I owed these doctors a courtesy visit.

The Philosopher was sniffing something from a vial of handblown glass. Dark powder dusted his nose.

"Want some?" he said. "It's a new synthetic."

"Cunt's out of control," said the Mechanic. "Making his own yay-yo, to hell with the world."

"Oh, piss off, Blackie," said the Philosopher. "Just a little pick-me-up."

These were not the dashing scientists of the amphitheater. The Philosopher was unshaven and looked long unwashed. His lab coat was covered with cobalt smears. The Mechanic had developed a tic of the eye that might have seemed lewd had the psychic deterioration which motored it not been so plain.

"Galileo," said the Philosopher through hinges of spit, "why have you forsaken me?"

"Cunt's dreaming of Pisa," said the Mechanic. "Can't see the truth of the situation. We got busted. We ran a scam and we got busted. I told him the mammoth bit was too much. Stupid. We could have had our own disease. Now we have squat. You can't patent death, I told him. You can't copyright a fucking nonstate, let alone the extinction of a species. Especially ours. Didn't I say this? I said this."

"So, am I dying or what?" I said.

"God revealed it to me," said the Philosopher, "yet now I must defy God to appease the church. I shall perish from the hypocrisy . . ."

"That film, that idiotic film," said the Mechanic. "Somebody's cousin with an educational library. Dumb. Dumb, dumb, dumb. So now we have what? What do we have now? The answer is C: Squat. Squat is the correct answer. We had everything going for us. The two names, perfect. You need two names for a good disease. Goldfarb-Blackstone. A Jew and a white guy. What's not to trust? Can't be a conspiracy, right? I mean, sure it could be for some people, but we weren't planning on this being a black disease. They have no insurance, by and large. I mean, well, what I mean by that is by and large. I'm not a racist, you know."

"I didn't know that," I said.

"It's true."

"But what about me?" I said.

"What, you?"

"Yeah, me."

"Oh, you. No, you're dying. Sorry, kid. Hate to say it."

"Dying of what?"

"I don't know. We haven't figured it out yet. What did we call it? Whatchamacallit. Good enough name as any, I guess."

"But you said it was a scam."

"The scam was everything else. See, we just wanted to stick out from the others. What's wrong with that? A brand, you know? Brand recognition. Brand—what's the word—leverage. Something for people to worry about on the drive to work. Something for the pharmaceuticals to jump on, the comedians to joke about. PREXIS dot net. Lots of people die all the time from nameless, mysterious diseases. What, do we deal with even a fraction of the shit that goes on? The answer, by the way, is D: Less than a fraction of the shit. It's like all those murders. Most go unsolved."

"What murders?"

"Exactly."

"So, what am I going to do?"

"I don't know. Cry. Pray. Go see the castles of Scotland."

The Mechanic's eye began to spasm anew, as though straining to vomit some abominable vision. The Philosopher fondled himself on the sofa.

"Doctor, doctor," he sang, "gimme the news . . ."

"Consider yourself the luckiest guy in this room," said the Mechanic.

"But I'm dying," I said.

"But nothing."

I found new doctors, furnished myself with further opinions. They slid me through tubes, onto tables, gurneys, toggled instruments that seemed forged in sterile smithies somewhere, cold bays carved deep into germless rock. They siphoned me, decanted me, bottled and labeled me, my blood, my snot, my waste, whatever coursed through me or sat in me, vatted, casked, the distillations of the guts, the body's gurgling treatment plant. They called me back, called me in, peeked into the corridor, closed the door.

The one with the eyeglasses sighed as she slid them off.

The one with the mustache stroked the bristles into place.

The fat one farted, made a meek look.

"Who can be certain?" they all began. There was concurrence about the uncertainty of certainty. There was concurrence about me.

I was dying of something.

It had no name.

Nobody wanted to venture one now.

I thought about Greta. I daydreamed about Clarice. I wondered if their industry had a tradition of charity work. I sat at home with Cudahy waiting for the symptoms to declare themselves. There had to be symptoms. Death could not precede the symptoms. My symptoms were late bloomers, but bloom they must. They owed me that much, whatever tribe of misery they hailed from: trembling, confusion, amnesia, aphasia, fevers, nomas, blebs. Dizziness, fatigue. Labored breathing. Loosened bowels. Blindness, boils, bedsore'd ravings, sears, flares, wens. Who knew? Nobody had ever done this kind of dying. Oh pioneer, the Patient Zero, the Subject Steve, the me of my given name, the me of my given fate, the chump of mysterium, the presymptomatic simp.

Did I deserve it?

Sure, like you deserve it.

Maybe only for being born.

Maybe only for wanting to be.

Because I did want to be. I wanted to stick around, stay in play. Who doesn't? you ask. Some doesn't, I reply. Me, I'd been there before, the brink, the brink of the blank. I'd come close with Maryse, closer by my lonesome. I'd practiced noose knots, stocked up on pills and gin. Maybe I wasn't the most likely candidate, but I definitely rated dark horse in the auto-snuff sweepstakes. I'd lived enough days when the days didn't end fast enough, days so chock full of me.

But now all I could think was: Let me live! Banish me, shun me, shoo me away, argue me off, but let me fucking live!

Already I was nostalgic for my sorrows. I wanted to savor heartsmash again, desertion, distraction, desolate nights, all the aches and bruises, love's bunions, the mind's bum knee. My mouth watered for bitter fruit. My belly panged for crow. There were no disaffected daughters in the patent-pending nonstate, no wife-pilfering Williams, no medallions of pampered meat. There were no tax forms to fudge, no binges to regret, no sweet depletions of the soul. There was nothing save a nothingness shot through with utter nothingness.

I wanted to keep myself in the realm of somethings, even all the awful somethings.

I wanted the cure.

I got curatives. I got pills, chemical injections, cautious portions of radiation served up by aproned technicians, junior chefs in the kitchens of deep frequencies. I got everything everyone got for dying of everything else, of known killers, named decimations.

I was still insured and they had all sorts of notions at their disposal, long shots, Hail Marys to spare.

"Nothing to lose," was their mantra. "Everything to be gained."

Loss gained. Loss never paused. Nothing took. The pills, the shots, rays, they made me sick. The symptoms! The symptoms had arrived! I thinned, I curdled, I shed.

Cudahy nursed me, nurses doctored me, and all seemed for naught. I was some sort of deliquescing human unit shuttled between home sofa and hospital cot. I sipped nutritional shakes from tin containers, dribbled them out on bathroom tiles, Cudahy's shoes. It was Cudahy who stood by me, truly, in toilet stalls, in taxi lines, in vestibules of vague stink. Maybe we were bound together by the beet fields of our boyhood, or the sweaty secrets of our fathers. I didn't think too hard about it. I was too weak, too grateful. I'd sent Fiona home. I required a secret fiefdom of shamelessness now.

The Further Opinions admitted to varying degrees of bewilderment. A surgeon named Lovinger wanted to cut. She just appeared one day, a voluptuous phantom there in x-ray where I loitered in my paper smock.

"I want to gut you," she said, "get a look-see. I've got a hunch. I'm a good huncher. This conversation is just between us. I can cut like nobody's business. Can I cut you?"

"I don't know," I said.

"I'm your last best hope."

Lovinger laid her hands on my shoulders. Supple, milky hands. A tiny Hebrew letter on a chain swung above the slope of her breast. She said it stood for life. It looked like a little ski-lift chair. I pictured us in it, an Alpine idyll with my surgeon-lover, Lovinger.

"Okay," I said. "Let's cut."

I was borne off in a whirl of orderlies to the new meat ward. My suitemate was an old man, a warren of tubes, puffs of rotted hair. The skin on his face looked blasted underneath, blood bombs gone off in secret detonations. The Los Alamos of all of us. Other men, younger men, slightly less ravaged versions of him, sat grave and dainty on the edges of his bed.

"You're just here for the money," the man said. "Save your breath. It's all going to the Elks. And the black kids. I promised scholarships."

"Dad, we really should discuss this."

The old man turned to me. I saw arid eons in his eyes.

"Fathers and sons," I said.

"The daughters killed me, too. And the daughters-in-law. All of them. Everybody. Except the Elks. I extend my gratitude to the Elks. They made a place for me. Saturday nights, some cards, some laughs. I'm a businessman, but I never forgot where I came from. I used to go down to the tough schools and make speeches to the black kids. They understand hardship. I told them if they didn't get knocked up or join those machine-gun gangs I'd send them to college. Maybe it's a waste, but if we get one good fellow out of it, one Washington Irving, it'll all be worth it."

"Dad, please."

"The papers are drawn up, Randy. You're Randy, right?"

He put out a crusted hand. The nearest son took it, started to cry.

"Christ," said the old man, "what I wouldn't give for a tough black son."

I slid out of bed, stood.

"Where you going?"

"I smell encroaching nothingness," I said.

"I know what you're smelling," said the old man. "It's not my fault. It's because the girl hasn't come. I keep pushing the button and she never comes."

The surgeon Lovinger caught up with me in the lobby.

"You've got to let me cut," she said. "I've got us a room and everything."

Cudahy was waiting for me out on the curb. The taxi driver took us through the park.

"Detour," he said. "Parade."

"What parade?" I said.

"Landlord Day," said the driver. "See the float?"

A great papier-mâché tenement house was rolling down the avenue. Men in matching motor caps carried signs: "Rent Control Is Mind Control."

"It's all about the little man," said Cudahy.

"The little man?" said the driver.

"The little lord," said Cudahy.

There was an old movie on TV about android gladiators. It

was set in the future, the late seventies. Cudahy sat beside me, cubing feta cheese.

"You know," he said, " 'robot' is a Czech word. I can't remember what it means. Here, this came."

He pushed an open envelope across the cutting board, shrugged when he saw me rub at the vinegar stains.

Dear Enrollee:

This notice hereby notifies you that your health plan has reached its maximum amount of maximum expenditure. We want to thank you for being such a faithful and valued customer.

> *Sincerely,*
> *Fran Kincaid*
> *Accounts Representative*

"This," said Cudahy, knifing at the screen, "is where the android's faceplate comes off to reveal a menacing tangle of wires. It's like a simile for our technology-crazed society."

"Insurance company cut me loose," I said.

"You're better off. I don't have any coverage. Look at me. I'm fine."

"I was fine, too."

"Fran Kincaid," said Cudahy. "Accounts representative. What do you think old Fran is doing right now? Slipping into her home-from-work dungarees, whipping up a little din-din, maybe?"

"What?"

"I can almost smell it," said Cudahy. "Garlic potatoes. Yum. Another tough day at the office, and now Fran's unwinding with a little Chablis, calling her sister, the perennial grad student. 'So, what's up, sis?' 'Not much, how's by you, Fran?' 'Oh, the usual, bringing ruin down on the poor slobs of the republic.' Am I right? Fucking Fran."

"Who?" I said. "Grad student?"

" 'Look, sis,' " Cudahy went on, doing voices now, twitching up his mouth, " 'you've got to find something and stick with it. The rest of us Kincaids, we work.' 'Up yours, Fran, everything's so easy for you, you don't get my deal at all.' 'Mom was right about you, sis. You're not as smart or as pretty as you think you are, but not dumb and ugly enough to take care of yourself. It's sad, really.' 'At least I didn't marry what's-his-name.' 'At least I didn't fuck my high school trivia team coach.' 'Finger-fucked.' 'Titter titter. Mmm.' 'What are you cooking, Fran?' 'Garlic potatoes.' "

"Cudahy," I said. "Hey."

"What?"

"What are you doing?"

"I don't know. It just wells up in me sometimes."

It was the last thing I'd ever hear him say. I nodded off while the androids praised Caesar in transistorized Elizabethan, woke to a bad stench. Cudahy's beautiful heart must have blown on a sprint to the john. His pants were at his ankles. I'd never noticed how hairy and slender his ankles were. All that grunt and shove of him rising up from those tender stalks. A new roll of toilet paper lay near his hand. I turned Cudahy over, saw a bubble on his lips. The bubble probably meant he was still breathing. Somebody said that, later. I sat there with his bright enormous head in my lap.

. . .

"What words could even begin to capture the indomitable spirit of our beloved Cudahy?"

I'd rented out a so-called intimately priced room in the basement of Ferguson's Funerary. Now I stood beside a wreathed easel festooned with snapshots slipped from a binder I'd found under Cudahy's bed. Shot-putters, mostly, a few light-damaged Latvian brides.

"He was a huge man with a huge heart," I continued. "He had no coverage."

I looked out to Fiona, my only fellow mourner, apart from Ferguson. Somebody else loomed up in the shadows behind her, a tight bloat of a man in aviator shades. He must have sneaked in while I'd been fussing with the easel. His shirt looked damp from the sink, his white-yellow hair tucked beneath a vintage derby. A great berry-colored stain fell down his cheek. Fiona's new beau? A far-flung colleague of Cudahy? Some wet brain weeping at the wrong bier? Ferguson had hinted he could hire grievers. Maybe this freak was on the house.

"Welcome," I said. "Thank you for coming."

The stranger gave a nod of grim salute and I resumed my address, but as I started talking I got the odd sense he was taunting me somehow. His eyebrows pogo'd up past his sunglass rims. He did some herky business with his elbows. Tremors, I figured, tried to ignore it, prattled on for a while about the birches and the beet fields and the moth cocoons. Most of it went dead in my mouth. This wasn't any kind of eulogy, more like a pitch, a campaign presentation. Sell the suits on how you mean to sell the legacy. Keep it punchy. Avoid the coy. I wished I had some graphics with me, visual backup, some fresh data, too. What was the mourning-Cudahy demo, anyway? His folks were dead and his family scattered. I sputtered onward into Cudahy minutiae—shoe size, culinary proclivities—groped for a grace note, a tag.

"So long, Cud," I said.

I signaled Ferguson, a tiny man with a sun-peeled nose. Ferguson made for the urn, a Florentine, he'd called it earlier, flourishing his line of them, but the stranger beat him to it, lifted the lid, peered in.

"What the hell are you doing?" I said.

"Not really what you'd call ashes. There's bone chunks in there."

"I'm going to have to ask you to leave," I said.

"When, man?"

"When what?"

"When are you going to ask me to leave?"

"Now," I said. "Leave."

The stranger made a gentle scooping noise in his throat, prelude to a loogie.

"Don't," I said.

"Lovely service," he said. "Very moving."

"You're in deep shit, son," said Ferguson. "I do cop funerals."

"You don't scare me because you're so midgety," said the stranger. "Are you aware of how midgety you are?"

"Please," said Fiona. "Please leave."

The stranger regarded Fiona with not a little tenderness. He tipped his sunglasses down to maybe do something cunning with his eyes. The stain on his cheek had a glittery quality.

"I'm Dietz."

"Fiona," said my daughter.

"Tell your father over there I have a message for him. The only cure is the disease."

"All right," I said. "That's it. Get out of here. Go."

"Relax," said Dietz.

"I'll relax when I'm dead," I said.

"That's original. Just remember what I said."

"What did you say?"

"Goddamn," said Dietz, and all his swagger seemed to drain from him at once.

He smacked at his head with the heel of his palm.

"You don't remember what you just said."

"I told them I wasn't ready for the people world."

"What are you talking about?" I said.

"The fucking clusterfuck is what I'm fucking talking about."

Dietz froze for a moment, then broke into a dead run out of the room. Ferguson locked the door behind him.

"I'm sorry, sir," he said, "I thought he was a friend of the deceased."

"It's okay."

"If I'd known he was going to pull a stunt like that I would have booked him a seat on the pain train."

"You?"

"I used to be a jockey," said Ferguson. "It's all just in the knees. You should see what I can do to a coconut."

"Do you need money?" Fiona asked me on the cab ride home. "How much was the cup?"

"It's called an urn," I said. "Who was that guy?"

"Forget him," said Fiona. "Probably busted out of some psych ward. Where'd you get the cake for the urn?"

"Cake? You sound like a venture capitalist with a coke habit."

"I was dating one for a while. During the boom."

"I don't want to hear about it."

"Of course you don't. Look, it's not my fault I had an early puberty. I didn't put the hormones in the milk supply."

"Can't I just not hear about it?"

"Here you are not hearing about it. Happy?"

"Within parameters," I said.

"So?"

"Cudahy had some cake on him. I used most of it for the cup."

"I can borrow from Mom."

"I wouldn't hear of it."

"William's loaded."

"William fulfills."

"I'm serious."

"I'm sure you are. Why don't I just move in with them?"

"I'll ask."

"I'm kidding."

"I'm not. Daddy, you're very sick. You need people around."

"What about you? I thought you were going to take care of me."

"I'm in a weird transitional place, right now. I don't think my presence would be good for either one of us. I need space to work it all through."

"Work what through?"

"My hatred for you."

"You hate me?"

"I didn't say that," said my daughter, diddled her pock.

I sat up the night with Cudahy's vodka, his videotapes. Shoot-outs, showdowns, duels in the sun. Frontier dust and destiny. No transitional spaces or places. Nothing to work through. Draw. Slap leather. Fill your hand. Cudahy believed in that kind of clarity.

Never could myself.

When Fiona was born I worried about the bills, my paternal deficiencies, my potential usurpation in the eyeshine of my wife.

"You are blessed," said Cudahy.

When I made team leader I grew furtive, paranoid, teased out every encounter for portents of sedition.

"Relax," said Cudahy, "you're a winner."

When Maryse left me, Cudahy drank to her riddance. Then he drank a shitload more and confessed to having loved her and even licking her ear one Thanksgiving while she tested the yams with a fork.

"There was a negligible amount of ass play, too," he said.

The truth was I knew all about it, but I let Cudahy confess and I forgave him. Forgiveness, like sin, is maybe just a matter of dwindling alternatives. Hell, it was only an ear, some ass, and Cudahy was no William, either.

We ended the evening of his confession in a bear hug under boulevard lights. Maybe we were both thinking of our fathers there in our boozy embrace.

This last we didn't discuss.

I cried for the both of us now, big vodka weeps. I draped

myself in Cudahy's track suit, those Valhallan warm-up duds, fell asleep while a bearded coot on the tube paid out a mine shaft fuse.

"This'll fix 'em," the coot cackled.

I dreamed I was the dialogue coach at the mine shaft location.

"No, really cackle it," I instructed the coot.

Later I dreamed my body had become a kind of cavern, too. Gypsy moths fluttered by the hundreds in my obsidian belly, drove clouds of wing dust up my stone throat.

Cudahy's dream likeness walked across the black pools and guano mounds of me. He had a gold Zippo, a can of my mother's HairNet spray. Wild gouts of fire rippled from his hands.

"Relax," said Cudahy. "You're a goner."

I woke up and reached for a water glass. The coaster beneath it unfolded, effloresced, a time-lapse flower.

Do you number among the Infortunate?

Did I number?

I numbered.

I dialed right down.

Items #3

The driver of the van said his name was Old Gold. He was a hairy kid with big crooked hands. Stuck on, those hands looked, maybe just for our drive. The van appeared to be a patch job, too. Mismatched doors, a yard-sale grille, a gummy coat of grayish paint. Bucket seats were bolted down where a banquette must have been. There wasn't much else. Stacks of blankets, some clementine crates. The floor was rotted through in places. You could look between your shoes, see bits of road.

"Thanks for the ride," I said.

Old Gold said nothing, aimed us toward the tunnel mouth. These ancient gullets under the river tended to unnerve me.

Too much speed for a burrow-lover. No warm dirt. I longed for the peace of an upward grade, us spit back to surface air, countryside, the towns. The van bucked through the greasy-tiled tube. Sandhogs, those were the men who built these things. I'd seen shows on the history station. Some got buried under bad walls with their bologna sandwiches. Progress, the crime. Progress, the cable premiere.

"Think she'll hold up?" I said.

"Who's that?"

"This baby," I said, patted the steering column.

"No touch," said Old Gold. "No touches."

"Sorry," I said.

We eased up into daylight and I noticed thin starbursts of scarring along his eyebrow, the near hinge of his jaw.

"Are you a boxer?" I said.

"When I was a kid," said Old Gold, "my father nailed an oak board up on the kitchen door. We had to hit it ninety-eight times with each hand before supper."

"Ninety-eight?"

"A hundred, I think the lesson would have been lost on us."

"I think I understand."

"I fought Clellon Beach once."

"Never heard of him."

"You were never in the Navy."

"That's true," I said.

"I knew it was true when I said it," said Old Gold. "I don't need your affirmation. I've been mothered by fire."

"What?"

"Nothing," said Old Gold.

We drove north in new silence. Factories into farmland into forests, forest towns. We made a pit stop near a place called

Mapesburg. Old Gold bought gasoline and a twin-pack of cup-cakes, laboratory pink.

"You're not a veganite, are you?" he said.

"A what?"

"Because these, I believe, originate in Alabama. You know, hydrogenated."

"These are fine," I said.

"Oh," said Old Gold. "You're one of those."

"One of what?"

"Fine, fine. Everything's fine, dear. No, trust me, I'm fine."

"I have no idea what you're talking about."

"So, you're an I-have-no-idea guy, too. Not an uncommon combo, come to think of it."

"Hey," I said. "Cut it out. This is crazy."

"You want to know what's crazy?" said Old Gold. "Climb-ing into the ring with Clellon Beach. That's fucking crazy."

He threw the van into gear, gunned into good, easy speed. I felt strangely calm. I'd always been a gifted passenger. Bliss in my boyhood had been the backseat, that foliate blur, the folds of my father's neck, the way my mother, our "navigator," twisted around with her maps and her snack mix, lowered each sodium-enhanced doodad into my hand with the gravity of ancient rite.

Our family had a tradition of bleak getaways. We were al-ways lighting out for some cold rocky coast. My father would walk out on a seawall, stand there with his arms crossed in what I took to be the existential defiance of certain dust jacket photographs. He worked for a home appliance company, wrote and edited operating manuals for juicers and drills and electric ranges, so a more gloried relation to the word might have been on his mind. Or maybe he was mulling a plunge, icy respite from life's dips and dives. Eventually he'd amble—even haunted he was one of the few legitimate amblers I've ever known—back to where my mother and I shivered on a tartan blanket, her conjuring the tidal chop in charcoal on a window-sized sketch pad.

"All my pretty ones," my father would say. "Fuckeroo'd."

I'd laugh. It was a funny word.

"Fuckeroo'd," he'd say again, and it wasn't that funny anymore.

Maybe the man had a feeling for the coming whammies. Like my mother falling in love with his cousin Manny, a guy who tended to brag about his Caddie's "nigger-locks," and her moving out to Arizona to help him run a profitable vanity press, lending her editorial hand to such titles as *Tao Jones: A Poem Cycle* and *Favorite Recipes from the Mossad*.

It wasn't just that she'd ditched him for his kin, either. Worse for my father, I think, whose mightiest praise was contained in the word "pro"—"You know, that paperboy, the Mickelson kid, he's a real pro"—she and Manny were now at the service of the amateurs, the no-talent fatheads with money to burn.

"Manny's never even read a fucking book," said my father. "Now he makes them."

"Hey," I said, home from school for the weekend, "the Wright Brothers never flew until they built a plane."

"Your flip college-boy remarks aren't helping," said my father. "I'm in a lake of fire here."

Still, my mother was my mother. I couldn't just forget all the hugs, the kisses, the granola and caramels. I took no sides over the years, or, rather, took both sides for whatever gain there was for a grown man. A few times I flew out to Phoenix with Fiona and we'd all sip fresh lemonade by the swimming pool.

"Your father hates me," my mother said once. "It's eating him up, I can tell. It's terrible. He needs to move on. Honey, if Maryse ever leaves you, remember to move on. Don't let it eat you up."

"I'll take care of him, Grandma," said Fiona.

"Do you people know something I don't?" I said.

"Hypothetical," said my mother.

"Just a scenario," said Fiona.

This mother and daughter were like sisters sometimes, doting on each other, turning on each other, teaming up. It was quite a thing to see. When that desert sun got in my mother's eyes and she did a head-on with an oil truck, I saw a lot of the light go out of Fiona. Some people get the lesson a little too early.

We flew out for the service, sat by the pool one last time, drank lemonade from a powder mix. Manny had locked himself in his Cadillac. He was hidden, mostly, but we heard his sobs, saw his boat shoes poke up past the dash.

"So, that's it?" said Fiona. "The whole thing's just a pile of random bullshit?"

"Some people," I said, "believe there's a purpose to it all."

"What, you mean like Heaven?"

"Some people," I said.

"Those would be the idiots, right?"

"I was raised to believe that those were the idiots, yes," I said. "But who knows?"

"Not fucking Grandma," said Fiona.

"Nobody can be sure," I said. "Have you ever heard of Pascal's wager? He said you might as well believe in God because if you don't, and God exists, you're screwed."

"Is that in the *Pensées*?"

"The what?" I said.

"He sounds like a chickenshit," said Fiona.

My father lost his mind with grief for the wife he'd already lost. Then he found another wife. I guess I wasn't as welcoming to Wilhelmina as I could have been. Maybe I begrudged him his new stab at happiness. I'd gotten used to the shell of the man and didn't necessarily wish the man back. It all came to some kind of head, though I can't quite remember what kind. I do recall my father's hand on my neck and a sliver of boiled leek on his lip. It's that father-son stuff. So much moist, fierce quivering muddies the picture sometimes.

My father moved to Pittsburgh with Winnie and now I got cards in the card seasons, snapshots of his duplex, his new felonious brood. Sometimes Fiona would visit him, file reports.

"He's deeply involved with a pen nib collector's club," she told me once. "The club has religious overtones but he won't reveal them. His sons—these would be my uncles, I gather— drop cinder blocks from highway overpasses. Winnie, as you know, is much younger, Amway pretty. She told me I was a winter girl in autumn colors."

"Dad," I said. "Oh, Dad."

"That's just what I always say," said Fiona.

"Feels good, right?"

I hadn't told my father I was dying. I was afraid he'd say what he always said by the seawall.

"My dad didn't have anything like a punching board," I

said to Old Gold now. "He tried to make me tough in other ways."

"Funny, I don't remember inviting you to compare our childhoods. Anyway, there's nothing to compare. I've been mothered by fire."

"Why do you keep saying that?" I said.

"Bears repeated repetition."

I looked out the window, watched the world unspool. Guardrails, guardrail rivets, mile markers, thruway kill. We were in high country and I was glad of it, patches of spruce and plowed fields in the valley below us, dark hills ahead. Up here, all this majesty, maybe you could just convince your flesh to reconsider.

I took out the brochure for the Center for Nondenominational Recovery and Redemption. The man who'd answered the phone the day before had been rather brusque. I heard wet noises, the snap of form-fitting rubber.

"Director here," he said.

We made vapid talk about upstate counties. Mostly I just listened to his voice. He had a good one, easy, kind of reedy, like a talk show host people go out of their way to persuade you is smart. I started to trust it, that voice, trust him. I wanted to fill up the void with my trust.

"Look," I said. "I don't know who you are or what you do, but I won't beat around the bush. You say you have the cure. If it's rat guts under my armpits, I'm willing to give it a whirl. Crystals and chanting, praying, tonal healing, whatever it is, I'll do it. I've read your brochure, and I've got to say, in my best days I'd be laughing my ass off. But things are a little different now. Good old Western know-how seems to have shit the bed.

Everyone says I'm a goner but no one can tell me why. So, now, I ask you, a total stranger, what should I do? Tell me. Please. Consider me your willing victim."

"I think you have the wrong number."

"Is this Heinrich?"

"This is the director."

"May I speak to Heinrich?"

"You are speaking to Heinrich. You are doing nothing else but speaking to Heinrich."

"You wrote me a note."

"Yes, I did. I saw you on the E.T.E."

"The what?"

"The electronic thought eliminator."

"The electronic—"

"The television."

"You wrote me a note. Someone brought it to my house."

"That would be Naperton."

"Okay, Naperton brought the note. All I know is that you said you had the cure. I've got it right here. 'I have the cure.—H.' I deduced that the H stood for Heinrich."

"Wonderful deduction," said Heinrich. "You really are a wonderful deducer."

"I'll let that slide," I said.

"Of course you will."

"How about we get real for a minute," I said.

"I'd advise against that."

"What's the cure, Doc?" I said.

"I'm sorry," said Heinrich. "But I'm not a doctor, and, as I may have stated earlier, you have the wrong number. You seem to be in search of a miracle. I don't traffic in miracles. And I don't associate with victims."

"Then what do you do, if I may be so bold as to ask?"

"Bold? Don't be ridiculous. All I'm sensing from you is a man who doesn't want to die. That's the deadliest condition of all."

"I've had my fill of philosophers," I said. "I guess you're right, I do have the wrong number. I thought you wanted to help."

We hung there for a while.

"Wait," said Heinrich, finally. "It's not your fault you're so faulty."

"Thanks for that."

"There'll be a supply van coming back to the Center from the city tomorrow. You can catch a ride."

"How much is this going to cost me?" I said.

"Cost you?" said Heinrich. "Why, everything."

"Maybe I should tell you now, I'm broke."

"I understand," said Heinrich. "It's not a problem. Money helps, but it's not a requirement. I'm talking about everything else."

"Sounds like you've got a cult up there."

"Everything's a cult, son. If it's not a cult it's a man sitting alone in a room."

"And in return I get cured?"

"Possibly. Or perhaps what you get is a brief moment of recognition before you pass into nothingness, which technically one cannot really pass into, it being a nonstate, but which I phrase this way for practical reasons."

"Given a choice, I'll take the cure," I said.

"Given a choice, he says," said Heinrich.

. . .

Now the sun was just another money shot behind the mountain tops. Old Gold bore down on the wheel.

"I hate twilight," he said.

"How long have you been at the Center?" I said.

"Three years. I'm in the 'Lives' part of the *Tenets*, even. 'Old Gold Speaks.' Wrote it myself, except for the spelling. Estelle did the spelling."

"Three years," I said. "Long time."

"Is it? I wouldn't know. I know that if I blink I'll miss infinity."

"That's deep," I said.

"Mothering fire'll melt the smartass right off of you," said Old Gold.

"Can't wait. So, do you know Heinrich well?"

"I know him."

"What's he like?"

"Clementines."

"Excuse me?"

"He likes clementines."

It must have been near midnight when we hooked hard onto a gravel road. It had begun to rain and Old Gold hit the high beams, hacked the liquid dark.

"Almost home."

We drove up to a metal gate. A man in a wet suit fiddled with some padlocks. Old Gold rolled the window down.

"Brother Bob," he said. "At it again, huh?"

The man held up his hand.

"Might as well cut the bitch off," he said.

We drove on through the compound, pulled over by a rain-rotted cabin.

"This is you," said Old Gold.

"You sure?"

"The Virgin Suite."

The cabin was dry, lit low with a Coleman lantern. An old stove stood in the middle of the room, kindling in a basket beside it. Part of the cabin seemed claimed, the bedsheets mussed, boots and socks stuffed under the cot. Candle wax puddled thick on a card table, and on a notebook open to a blank page. A piece of hemp rope dangled down from a rafter beam.

My end of things was fairly bare. A blanket, a bath towel, a cot, a moldy bedroll with a book wedged in the twine. There was a note in the book, scrawled on a swatch of grocer's paper. *The only cure is the cure. —H.* I balled up the note. Cutesy tautologies would herewith be tossed beneath the cot. Now I took up the book, a dark hardback with embossed lettering: *The Principles and Tenets of Nondenominational Recovery and Redemption*, by Heinrich of Newark.

It was some sort of compendium of community rules—numerated, bulleted, with footnotes, appendices. Towards the back was a section called "Lives Lived and Redeemed," a brief table of contents: "The Ballad of Estelle Burke," "Dietz Versus Dietz," "Notes on Naperton." I flipped ahead to a chapter called "Old Gold Speaks":

Listen, I fought Clellon Beach in a Navy smoker and I can tell you that man was a huge fucking killer. It's a wonder I didn't die from his blows. Before Clellon I was just your average country Jewboy with tough hands from hitting the kitchen board and not thinking of all the things my daddy did to me mentally and on the physical side to prepare me for the world, but what world? His world? He had a sick one. When Clellon did up my skull the way he did with the quickest combos you've ever seen, or really that you've never seen (they were that quick), I spent a month in the base infirmary hooked to the life machines and it was here that all the poison gas seeped out of the safe part of my brain and poisoned me up through to the gills. I was a walking time explosion even before I could even walk again. Then I read this book (well, probably not the very copy you're holding) and I found in The Director's words something to live up to for. I went then to embark on my pupilage under him and have gone through the phases of awareness and have been mothered by fire and have delivered myself unto myself and I am a hero and a cloudwalker and I don't blame Clellon for my bad lives but he's a hero, too, and someday there will have to be a reckoning of us because that is the lost way of men and women from back in the age of continuum. Oh, and Old Gold was my Navy nickname only. My real name is Avram Cole Younger Gold."

Cloudwalkers? Continuum? This was the cure? I dimmed the Coleman down, stretched out on the cot, awaited my symptoms, what I now considered my symptoms. They tended to muster at night, those nervy shoots and shudders I used to figure for the natural rot of me.

I'd had a cancerous aunt who went to Guam for a medical miracle—it's how I knew about the rat guts—and she came back flush with remission. She died the next spring but I'm pretty sure her excursion bought her another season of precious decay. Maybe the difference was that they knew what was killing her. Me, I was dying of something no one had ever died of before.

Maybe Heinrich could name it.

Or at least write a new section of the *Tenets* called "Lives Lost."

Now I did something I hadn't done in a while. It felt good in my hand, throbbed there like some wounded bird you've just found in the woods. I cast Greta and Clarice in a stroke number based on material from another medium, pictured jets of gaudy lady juices piped out of Vegas fountains. Jennifer Applebaum, whose solitary nipple hair had enslaved my senses for a year of junior high, appeared now unbidden in a fur stole. Even Maryse had a caustic winning walk-on.

Harem arrayed, I came like Xerxes back from giving it to the Greeks. I let what spilled dry to a new skin on my fingers, fell off into a dream about figs.

"Somebody got some."

The man from the gate sat on the far cot in a paisley robe and a watchman's cap. He looked my age, a little younger. Boyish, worn by the linger of his boyishness. He pointed oddly at me now. It seemed I'd kicked away my blanket in the night. My pants were at my knees, my hand doing make-work down past my belly, some idle, half-asleep flippering.

"Bachelor habits," I said.

"Me," said the man, "I'll lie in bed, do it all day. Won't get up till the dinner bell. Then I get disgusted with my regression and I must impose strictures. Sign up for extra chores. Won't touch myself even to wash it. I'm Bobby. Bobby Trubate. The real one. Actual size."

"Glad to meet you," I said.

"You'd be Steve," said Trubate.

"That's not really my name," I said.

Trubate set his cap on the pillow, felt with his fingers along his skull.

"Ever take your hat off but then it feels like it's still on?"

"Nerve endings," I said.

"You a nervologist? What if it's some supernatural force pushing down on my head? Something your science can't explain."

"Anything's possible," I said.

"Oh, you think so?"

"Within parameters."

"Well, I guess it's my duty to welcome you to the land of the Infortunate. Come on, it's almost time for First Calling."

Trubate led me out into the mudshine, the morning. We walked past a row of cabins thrown up on either side of the rutted track. The walls were rough timber with some patches of plywood, tin. The compound stood partway up the mountain on a terraced clear. Below us, where the forest steepened to the valley floor, buildings sloped down both banks of a river, near a high steel bridge.

"That's Pangburn Falls," said Trubate. "The de facto town. Some of the old-timers used to go down to Pangburn, but not since Wendell died. Have you read 'The Wanderer Wendell' yet?"

"No."

"An inspiring text."

"I didn't see anything about a Wendell in that book," I said. "Or you."

"I haven't earned canonization just yet. I'm only in the

early middle phases of continuum awareness. I haven't been mothered by fire. But I'm taking notes. I want my Life to be stylistically innovative. Like my work on the silver screen."

"I'm sorry," I said, "I'm not familiar with your work."

"Sure you are," said Trubate.

"I don't think so."

"You've seen me a million times. The junkie, the junkie car jacker, the corrupt senator's junkie son. I do them all. 'Who was that guy?' you wondered. 'He's good.' I'm that guy. I am good. I'm a fucking craftsman."

"I don't get to the movies much," I said.

"Yeah, you go read to the blind every night."

"I've done that."

"Sick fuck."

"What are you talking about?"

"You think they want to be reminded?"

Now the track curved down a bit.

"There's the dining hall," said Trubate, nodded down the hill at a clapboard building the size of a country church. "The chicks sleep in that wing sticking off."

"I didn't know there were any," I said.

"It's mostly dudes up here. It used to be all-dude. Because of our increasingly chick-run society and all. But Heinrich had an epiphany on that, so now there are exceptions. That's his crib, by the way, right down there."

Near the dining hall was another cabin, the only one I'd seen with a porch.

"Who built this stuff?" I said.

"Read the *Tenets*. Over there are the barns. We have a bunch of milking cows. Naperton runs the farm. We make a damn tasty organic cheese spread. Sell it down in the city. Have you ever put your hand in a newborn calf's mouth? It's amazing. Sensuous, yes. Erotic, sure. But not dirty. Not at all. And up there through the hill trail is the mothering hut. I wouldn't worry about that now. Your time will come. We're all very excited about the project."

"What project?"

"Sorry, that's the old me talking."

"I don't see the fence," I said. "Where's the fence?"

"What fence?"

"You were there last night. At the gate. With a lock."

"Yes, I was. I signed up for gate duty last week. Penance, I guess. Not that I'm religious, just a fucking pig."

"So," I said, "if there's a lock, and a gate, where's the fence?"

"Why in the world would there be a fence? We're not convicts."

"But there's a gate."

"You've got to have a gate. What else are you going to arrive through?"

Down below us the dining hall door skidded open. People made their way across the lawn to Heinrich's porch. We jogged down the slope to join them, fell in with Old Gold. Nearby a woman and a teenage boy who shared enough odd jut of nose and jaw to pass as mother and son talked heatedly. Others poured in now from all parts of the compound, some limping, some severely bent. The Infortunate seemed to specialize in warped bones and voided stares. They rolled out straw mats on the grass or just squatted there, diddling the moss, decapitating dandelions, muttering at the sky. A man in a derby kneaded the neck of a young woman in a wheelchair. She was fat and beautiful with a swoop of henna'd hair. The man caught me staring, tipped his hat brim up. I saw the berry-colored stain on his cheek.

"Dietz," I called to him.

He looked at me darkly.

"Dietz," I said. "Do you remember the message?"

"Who's that?" the woman asked him.

"A people," said Dietz. "A people who needs to relax."

"How's the clusterfuck?" I called.

"Cool it," said Trubate, slung me toward a patch of grass.

Now the porch door swung open and a man in a hunter's vest angled up to the rail.

"Naperton," I whispered.

"You know him, too?"

"He knows me."

Naperton drummed his clipboard, peered up at the sky.

"Good morning, morning!" he said.

"Good afternoon!" said the gathering. They spoke as one in a somewhat feverish singsong. Here and there, perhaps, were hints of sedition, or at least drill-weariness, but most of the Infortunate sounded sincerely joyful, near exultant, insane.

"Evening is upon us somewhere!" said Naperton.

"Good morning, evening!"

"The past is before us!"

"We're coming, past!"

"The future is gone!"

"Fare thee well, future!"

"Now is . . ."

"Now!"

"Now is . . ."

"Now!"

"I am . . ."

"Me!"

"I am . . ."

"Me!"

"And who are you?" called Naperton, pointed out to the crowd.

"I am me, me am I!"

Old Gold jammed his head into the earth, jerked himself up into some kind of ecstatic teeter. He stabbed out his hands and made banshee noises. Some clapped in time to his spasms, his war whoops. It was hard to tell if this was encouraged. Others pinched their eyes and puled. Dietz looked out from beneath his hat with an expression of bored expertise. Trubate rocked beside me, rapt. Old Gold tipped back to the grass, sunlit beads of spittle on his lips.

"I am me," he said. "Me am I. I ma me. I me ma. I ma me ma I."

"Well done!" called a voice.

There was a new man at the rail. He had hair of wavy silver, thick country arms, wore dungarees, a dirty dress shirt. He looked like a midwestern math teacher, a professor with a hobby garden. I knew at once it was Heinrich. Some calm of the high ordinary pulsed out of him, soft, metronomic, a charisma of reduced noise.

"People," he said quietly now, "I have something to impart to you. A fable, if you will. It concerns a lonely zookeeper and the beautiful, fiercesome tigress who fell into his charge. When I say lonely I mean lonely, okay? The zookeeper, I mean. So picture it, an anonymous little fellow, no friends, no family, no love. Nothing. Picture a poor little man whose most intimate conversations take place over cash registers, at salad bars, or in the bathroom mirror. Are you picturing it? It's important that you picture it. This is what we call in the biz guided imagery. It's still very big in the biz right now, this guided imagery thing. So, picture it, okay? Loneliness. Loneliness of the unrelenting variety. Understand, I'm telling you all this not to embarrass this man, who exists only on the plane of parable, anyway, but rather in what you would have to grant is an honest go at character development. Because I believe in character development. People, you should never consider me not in agreement with the idea of character-driven image-guided parable. But we're off the beaten track, here, really. We're far afield the ground-down path. What I want you to picture, really, for parable's sake, is this lonely zookeeper whose only companion is the beautiful and fiercesome tigress who has fallen into his charge. Because, and this is important, the motherfucker couldn't take his eyes off that cat. Motherfucker was in love with that stripey bitch. Unnatural? Okay, sure, unnatural. I don't even know what natural is, people. Not in this world. And I sure as hell am not going to lay a moral trip on you. Oh, I know, morality is so important these days. Our society, it's fracturing and fissuring and fragmenting and all the other f-words, too, all because of a lack of moral structure. Well, not on this mountain, people. You want slave morality, that's the next mountain over. This is Mount Redemption. This is my fucking mountain. Got it? Good. So, let's get back to our regularly scheduled parable. When last we left, our lonely zookeeper was lusting for the tigress who'd fallen into his charge. And let me tell you something, a lust like this makes room for calculation. So one night he shoots her with a tranquilizer gun and climbs into her cage. He gets down and holds her drugged-up head in his arms, kisses her, whispers in her ear, works himself up into a lather, a slaver. Do you like slaver better? Let me know. Drop your suggestions in the suggestion box. But in the meantime, listen to me. This zookeeper. He unzips his trousers, dig? He whips it out. He whips it out and does the deed. The deed. He does it. Dig?"

"We dig," called Old Gold.

"Okay, then," said Heinrich, his voice rising. "Deed done, the zookeeper sets his watch alarm to coincide with the duration of the sedative and snuggles up beside the cat. He sleeps a sleep he has never known before. A golden sort of sleep, the deep, dreamless slumber of the unvanquished. Unvanquished, as in yet-to-be-vanquished. Am I laying it on too thick? Maybe I'm laying it on too thick. But when, tell me people, when is it ever really thick enough? I've never once seen it thick enough. It's always too thin, isn't it? Too damn thin.

"Anyway, back to our sympathetic bestialist. Because a story like this depends on sympathy, so I advise you all to sympathize. Or empathize. Which is more sympathetic. Back to the zookeeper's frequent and clandestine mountings. Back to the unvanquished thickness of our golden empathy and the zookeeper's feline humps. Repeat once nightly for, oh, a week.

"So one evening the zookeeper is thrashed awake by the newly roused tigress, who lets loose a howl that could serrate the stars. You like that? Serrate the stars? I made that up. That's not in the original parable. But that's how these things work. Thousands of years of revision, refinement. I'm storytelling, here. We're gathered around the cookfire here. Fire, man. Pretty fucking exciting. Now the tigress, she howls, she leaps, and the zookeeper, he just barely rolls away from her wet snapping jaws, wriggles himself out of the cage. Just barely. Witness the zookeeper, bruised but intact. Intact, but scared out of his mind. Picture scared, people. Picture load-in-your-skivvies scared. Visualize, visualize.

"Whew! Can you say that, people? Whew? You can bet your ass the zookeeper said it. Whew!

"Never again, he vows. Never again. But the next day, hosing down her cage, she appears to him almost coy, lazing there in the afternoon heat, and it seems to him that with those sultry squints of her tigress eyes, those drowsy paw strokes on her smooth belly, that sexy way her feline spittle ropes out of her mouth, maybe she's . . . well, it's just a hunch, but maybe, I mean couldn't she actually be acknowledging their tryst, or, can you believe it, assenting to it! Why not? thinks the zookeeper, which I say for the sake of fable, for in truth no man can say for sure what another thinks, especially someone who doesn't exist. Still, hell, why not? Their love is forbidden in her kingdom too, right? It's probably just as thrilling.

"The zookeeper, however, is not unwary, so that night he returns to her cage door with a double dose of cat tranks locked and loaded. He draws a bead on her exquisite rump, but finds himself unable to pull the trigger. He shudders to imagine the shock of the needle piercing her hide. He dreads that baleful look on her face as the chemicals creep through her system and shut her down in stages.

"We are lovers now, thinks the zookeeper, we have built a trust. Or at least a tryst. So Zoo-man tosses the gun away and strips off his uniform, enters the cage armed only with his otherworldly tumescence. Do you all know what a tumescence is?"

"A tumessens!" called Old Gold. "That's a boner!"

"Nothing but, young Avram," said Heinrich. "Nothing but.

So here we got Mr. Lonely Zoo-man with his parable-derived, parabolic boner looking down on the object of his love, the winsome, ferocity-graced tigress.

"Come to Daddy, zookeeper coos.

"But does Tigress come to Daddy? Does Tigress bend to Daddy's whim? Fuck no! Tigress leaps! Tigress pounces! Bitch munches him up!

"And as the zookeeper lies bleeding to death, he sees it, his tumessens, if you will, now a pale tiny thing pinched in his pawed lover's maw.

" 'Why?' moans the zookeeper. But as he twitches there in the corner of the cage, he remembers another ancient and oft-cited ditty about a frog and a scorpion and a not dissimilar breach of trust, and suddenly he knows perfectly well why."

"It's a fable within a fable!" said Old Gold.

"Avram Cole Younger Gold, we have college boys here who aren't as sharp as you. You're damn right. Fables within fables. Wheels within wheels. Such is the way to wisdom. And to madness. But back to our story. The zookeeper remembers this other little number about a frog and a scorpion, or a tarantula and newt, or a salamander, it doesn't matter. And the zookeeper, now in his pulped puppety death throes, now in what the Teutons might call *der Todeskampf*, the zookeeper says, 'I understand, my love, I understand, I know why you did this. It's because you're a tiger. That's why, right?'

"Now the big cat leers at him, her flat eyes coins of a darker realm. You like that? Coins of a darker realm? I'm still tweaking that. But anyway, the tigress she looks at him, this dying zookeeper, she levels her leveling gaze at him.

" 'Listen, punk,' she says, 'the fact that I'm a tiger's got nothing to do with it. It's just that you got stingy with the good stuff.' "

I laughed. It was hard to tell if it was okay to laugh. I guess it wasn't okay.

"People," said Heinrich, "I want to welcome a newcomer among us. His name is Steve. Get up, Steve."

"I'm Steve," I said, and stood.

I waited for welcome, for hugs, finger gongs.

Nobody said a word.

"I'm Steve," I said. "Provisionally, I'm Steve, and I'm dying of something. Nobody knows what it is, but it's killing me. I don't want to die. That's about it. Thanks."

"Sit, Steve," said Heinrich.

Trubate tugged me to the ground.

"Seen worse," he whispered.

"There you have it," said Heinrich. "Provisionally Steve. A provisional man afraid to confront the truth. Pretty damn pathetic, ask me."

"Hey!" I said.

"Hey, what?"

"Where do you get off with this shit?"

"The question is," said Heinrich, "where do you get on? Or here's another: who are you?"

"I am me," I said, approximating Old Gold's quaver.

"Not yet, you're not. You're not shit."

I barely took in the rest of the meeting, my first First Calling. There was something said about illicit speech acts in the trance pasture, a tentative scheduling of the next cheese run, a note or two about revisions to the chore board. A kid named Lem, the one I'd seen bickering with his mother, was singled out for various community infractions. Heinrich passed a sentence upon him which I did not understand. Others shuddered. I started to wonder if I'd made a major mistake. I'd read about places like this in my father's stroke books, back in the grand old days of investigative porn. Depressed kid joins up with a guru, empties his checking account, splits for parts unknown. Feds find him chunked for canning in a mackerel plant. Friends note he was always kind of a follower. "Fuckeroo'd," says his father, Vice President of the Nibs of Nod.

Heinrich didn't end the meeting so much as abandon it, wander back into the porch shade. The gathering sat for a while, silent, like an audience savvy to the possibility of a trick ending. Then, in staggered waves of bravery, or boredom, they stood.

Lem's mother took my arm.

"I'm Estelle Burke," she said.

"But are you you?" I said.

"Don't take it so hard. When I was a little girl in ballet school the teacher was always toughest on the most promising students."

"Is that where you learned not to take it so hard?"

"I never learned," said Estelle. "I wasn't promising."

"Your boy seems to have gotten himself into some trouble," I said.

"Heinrich is Lem's father. Spiritually speaking, of course. He'd never do anything to harm Lem. Or me. I don't care what he says at First Calling."

"Bark is worse than his bite?"

"This has nothing to do with dogs," said Estelle.

"It's a saying," I said.

"Sayings say nothing," she said.

We crossed the lawn to the dining hall. Sun spilled down on long pine tables. Some morose-looking sorts were busing breakfast trays.

"Can I get some food?" I said.

"You'll have to ask Parish."

"Where's Parish?"

"I was expecting who's Parish."

"I'm on the quite-fucking-hungry side."

"You've been assigned to kitchen duty."

"Kitchen duty? I'm a sick man."

"Take a number."

"I'm not kidding."

"Who's kidding? Chores are sacred."

"What?"

"Read the *Tenets*."

"Everyone's really recommending that book," I said.

Parish the cook explained patiently that a missed meal was a meal missed. It was a fascinating theory. He was a hard little potato of a man in a tight pink T-shirt that read: *There are no shit jobs, just shit people*. His rhinestone-studded tool belt bristled with spatulas and slotted spoons. He pointed to a steel box bolted to the countertop.

"That's your new girlfriend," he said. "Keep her hot and wet and we'll all be happy."

The machine was easy, a push-pull job, just the kind of sweaty rote that maybe makes the doer dream of sickles on the Winter Palace steps, or cocoa-buttered asses in Daytona. I finished in about an hour, numbed by the slosh of water and tin.

A steam rash ran from my hips to my neck. I worried it, another symptom. I stood there with my shirt open, clawing the spread.

"It'll go away," said Parish.

He handed me a plate with pita bread, some runny cheese. "Just this once."

Out in the dining hall I took a table near a great stone hearth. Nailed above it was a double-handed saw, rusted, cracked in the grips. Flat on the mantel beneath it was a copy of the *Tenets*. I took it down and started to skim:

In the beginning was the bird, rotating me back to the late great forty-eight. After that, more service to the state, Uruguay, El Salvador, Pepsi, Bell. But why bore you with corpses, the assassin's litany? Suffice it to say I was one of those who made you safe and warm and free enough to ruminate upon your pain, an activity formerly restricted to aristocrats, and thus helped you along your poison path....

... And then it came to pass, late in the winter of 1982, that I met Notwithstanding "Notty" Naperton, ex–dairy farmer, in an upstate drunk tank. Upon release we reconvened at Ned's End Tavern for a breakfast of boilermakers, then retired to his room above a hardware emporium to wax incoherent about our disappointments, our regrets, our boats missed and doomed dinghies boarded. We were petty, hateful men and we both saw the world for the meaningless worm farm it was. We wondered what possible reason there could be to perdure. Now at this juncture Naperton confessed his clincher. The only thing that kept him on this earth, he told me, was the fact that an inoperable tumor had been detected in his brain. He was dying and he felt he had no right to intervene. Nonsense, Notty, I told him, we've been stripped of all possible actions save one. Suicide is the only uncompromised gesture left.

Even wasting away from a grapefruit brain is a kind of complicity in the nightmare of life, I argued, not to mention the fact that all variety of scum profit from your illness. Naperton was soon swayed. I, myself, had been contemplating the act for a long time. I'd snuffed enough lives in the employ of democracy to know that any idea of the preciousness of my own was pure affectation. At dawn we drove up to the place you stand now with a pair of pistols, fully intending to vacate our fleshly premises, and with no delusions about tenancy in any afterworld, either. We sat on the forest floor amidst the spruce needles and the pine cones and stared down our respective barrels. I suggested a three-count. Naperton complained that he'd left no suicide note. He had an ex-wife he claimed to still love who deserved explication. I told Naperton that the shape his diseased brain matter took on the tree trunk behind him would serve as ample explication. I commenced my three-count and Naperton let me reach two before he stopped me again. Tears were streaming down his face. "Wait," he said, "what if we lived?" I admonished Naperton to stop delaying the inevitable. I began to grow frustrated, as when certain Honduran activists had resisted my offer of an easy and silent termination. I considered disposing of the three-count altogether, also aware of the possibility that Naperton was in no condition to live up to his end of the bargain. I was about to waste the poor fuck and then attend to my own mortal self-infliction when Naperton's query suddenly struck something deep within me. A chord, I think they call it. "What if we lived?" Such a simple, and yet infinite, question. I looked around, took in the trees, the moss, the fungus nestled in fallen timber. I heard the tittering of birds, the rustle of life in the brush. Everything seemed puny and the puny things true. You could take possession of yourself in the tiny and mindless movements of this earth. You could start all over again. You would have to be birthed anew, without fear, without belief, without state, without civilization. You could be redeemed! Philosophy? Never! The despair of the philosophers was correct, their correctives patently false. I knew then that we would build something here. I laid the gun down and watched Naperton do the same. "Do you feel it?" I said. "Feel what?" said Naperton. "Your tumor," I said, "it's gone." Behold, subsequent diagnostic procedures proved it so!

And later:

... dopefiends, drunks, nutjobs, fools, terminal cases, melancholics, paranoiacs, chronic onanists, rapers of pigs, bad poets, etc.: This is your home. We have made for you a home. To live in our home you must forsake all others. This should not be difficult. You would not be here if you were welcome elsewhere, if you flowed without incident or complaint through the global circuitry of want. The world is pain and early death for most, Slurpees for some, wealth and ease for a very few. And as for that business about passing through the eye of a camel, or a needle, or whatever, don't believe it. Even now the elite are developing the right nanotechnology for the job. The Center for Nondenominational Recovery and Redemption was founded by Heinrich of Newark and Notwithstanding Naperton with the belief that the tired and the sick were getting a raw deal in our republic, sent off to the corner with a broken toy called God, or Goddess, or Higher Power, or inner peace. All modes have conspired against you. Take your place among us and deliver yourself unto yourself. We accept all major credit cards.

Now came a page entitled simply "The Tenets."

1. There is a vast gulf between those who have been mothered by fire and those who have not. Respect said gulf.
2. Periods in the trance pasture are mandatory.
3. Chores are sacred, prayers debased.
4. Televisions, radios, telephones, or any other devices designed for broadcast or communication to or from the given world are expressly forbidden.
5. God is dead. Godless man is dead.
6. Violence will be met with decisive violence.
7. You are you.
8. To each according to his culpability, from each according to his bleed.
9. We are spawn of woodland apes. No code has been undone. Neither faith nor reason will deliver us. We must look to the trees.

10. The given world has already calculated the potential worth of your unhappiness. No country, no religion, no corporation is your friend. No friend is your friend.

Now something damp and tentacled was doing a dance in my hair.

"It's your time to shine," said Parish.

He handed me the mop, pointed to a bucket on wheels. The water stank of some chemist's idea of the woods. I mopped the dining hall, tried to picture a New-and-Improved Pine-Scented Forest. Antibacterial spatterdock was just sprouting near a lake of lye when my eyes began to sting. I went to the kitchen to rinse them, found Parish peeling a kiwi.

"Good job," said Parish. "Don't forget to punch out."

He showed me how, dropped a slice of rye into an Eisenhower-era toaster. We waited for it to pop. There was a corkboard near the door, a spotty hunk of pumpernickel pinned to it.

"The problem," he said, "is that the punch bread rots."

"That would be the problem with punch bread," I said.

I hiked back up the dirt track to my cabin, found Heinrich lying on my cot.

"Power nap?" I said.

His eyes ticked past me toward the rafters.

"See that rope?" he said.

"Noticed it last night."

"Guy name of Wendell. Bunked here for a while. Of course he figured the drop all wrong. Strangled. That's usually how the do-it-yourselfers go. No time to learn the craft."

"Why did he do it?" I said.

"That's the question of a child, Steve, but I'll try to answer it. Wendell was a slave. But half free. The pain is too unbearable for a man like that."

"His family must have been upset."

"We were his family. We were upset."

Heinrich gripped the cot frame, vaulted off it.

"Your bunkmate," he said, "that Bobby. He talks too much. I adore him, but sometimes I worry he will never reach continuum awareness. I'm not worried about you."

"Maybe you should tell me what you're talking about before you decide not to worry."

"It's no big secret, Steve. Just try to remember the one or two moments in your life when fear broke for lunch. Quite a feeling, right? Now imagine feeling that way all the time."

"I don't think I have too much time left to feel anything."

"That's what Naperton thought."

"Behold," I said, "subsequent diagnostic procedures proved it so!"

Heinrich's punch landed somewhere in the vicinity of my liver. Next thing, I was performing a sort of fetal waltz across the floor planks.

Heinrich hovered near the door.

"I'm not saying it's great literature," he said, "but we take the *Tenets* pretty seriously around here."

I didn't hear him leave.

Dinner that night was some lewd stew I'd watched Parish concoct, undercooked carrots and pulled pork in ooze. I believe he threw some kiwi in there, too.

"All I know," he'd said, "is that there's got to be vat of something at the end of the day. That's all I know and all I need to know."

I served myself from said vat.

"Steve-o," called Bobby Trubate. "Join the kiddie table!"

He was sitting with the woman in the wheelchair I'd seen at First Calling.

"This is Renee," said Trubate.

There was another man at our table, balding, with bad skin, and jowly, I thought, until I noticed the good-sized goiter under his jaw. He'd outfitted himself as some kind of eighteenth-century European infantryman, down to the britches and boots, the leather cartridge box.

"That's DaShawn," said Trubate. "He's a Jackson White."

"I told you," said DaShawn, "I don't approve of that term."

I leaned in to Renee, pointed to where Dietz sat with Heinrich near the hearth.

"Your boyfriend banish you?" I said.

"My boyfriend?" she said. "Fuck you."

"She bites," said Trubate. "But does she swallow?"

"Fuck you, too, Bobby. Mr. Hollywood."

"Fuck Hollywood," said Trubate. "I'm not Hollywood."

"Let me try again," I said to Renee. "I'm—"

"Please don't try again. I know who you are, and this isn't some fucking singles retreat."

"Renee is muy sensitivo," said Trubate. "She knows guys like to hit on her because they think she's easy and they figure they're saints for doing it. And they can't help but wonder what it's like to ball a hot gimp. Hell, I wonder."

"You've really got me all figured out, Bob," said Renee.

"I'm so lucky to have a spokesman like you. Explaining my predicament can be so exhausting."

"See, she's touchy," said Trubate.

"She's right," I said.

"She's about to puke," said Renee, rolled off with her stew bowl in her lap. We watched her bump a nearby table, swivel, swear.

"They don't want your pity," said DaShawn. "They want ramps."

"She wants tunnels," said Trubate. "Wet warm ones."

"What?"

"Let's just say she's leased some serious property on the Island of Lesbos."

"Renee's gay," said DaShawn.

"Go ahead, use the clinical term," said Trubate.

"What's it to you?" I said.

"Oh, it's a lot to me," said Trubate. "What, are you some kind of tolerance cop? Look, guys want to fuck each other, that's cool with me. That's the Socratic Method, for God's sake. But chick on chick? I find that exclusionary."

"Exclusionary of you."

"Dude, obvo."

"DaShawn," I said, "where are you from?"

The lance corporal looked up.

"The Ramapo Mountains."

"Is that how they dress up there?"

"This is a replica of the uniform worn by Hessian mercenaries during your colonial war."

"My war?"

"I don't think the Founding Fathers had my kind in mind

when they penned their immortal words of liberty. We descend from a mixed breed of runaway slaves, Indians, and Hessian deserters. All enemies of your glorious republic."

"I don't remember signing anything," I said.

"He's the only Jackson White that ever went to college," said Trubate. "The rest of them live in little shit shacks with broken antennas on top."

"I'm not white and my name's not Jackson," said DaShawn. "They're cable-ready up there now."

"What brought you to the Center?" I said.

"What brings any of us?" he said.

"I'm here for a cure."

"DaShawn's here for that fucking egg on his neck."

"Grave's disease?" I said.

"Who doesn't have that?" said Bobby Trubate.

"We're working on my thyroid," said DaShawn. "Among other things."

"Good luck, pal," said Trubate.

"Cease transmission of negative ionic force, please," said DaShawn.

"He says that sometimes," said Trubate.

"I'm saying it now," said DaShawn, and stood, made for the bus cart with his plate.

"Why be such a pussy?" Trubate called after him. "You're already ugly and fucking insane. Why add to your problems?"

"You have such a way with people," I said to Trubate.

"I'm a truth-teller. That's how I ended up here."

"Just that?"

"Well, the speedballs, too. Don't you read the trades?"

"Not your trades."

"Right, I forgot. You're pretending I'm not a celebrity.

Well, doesn't matter. I've been in and out of lots of joints. My problem is the enormity of my talent. My manager suggested this place. Saw an ad somewhere. I haven't heard from him since. Good riddance, though. I'm into deep meaning now. Like I'd ever bother to do television again. Unless it was quality television."

Someone was tapping a water glass. I thought of all the flatware and silverware out here tonight I'd be on intimate terms with in the morning. Parish had been full of huzzahs for my hose work, said I possessed an intuitive form of the bubble dancer ethos: let no dirty or dirty-seeming thing pass through. Now the tapping got louder and the room hushed down. Heinrich rose before the hearth.

"People of recovery and redemption," he said, "I hope I speak for all of us when I say to our brother Parish in the kitchen, with regard to our fare tonight, well done, well done! But now we must move on to graver concerns, namely the execution of our sentence upon young Lem Burke for crimes against the community and egregious violations of the *Tenets*. Lemuel, if you will."

The boy stood.

"Please," he said softly. "Please, don't."

Estelle Burke howled from the doorway. Old Gold hooked her under the arms, gagged her while she kicked.

"Please," said Lem. "I promise I won't do it again."

"Won't do what again?"

"Those things."

"I'm afraid," said Heinrich, "that you have yet to exhibit any comprehension of your transgressions. Harness!"

It looked something like a rolling wardrobe rack. Naperton wheeled it into the room.

Lem was weeping now.

"Please, please don't."

"Disrobe!" said Heinrich.

Lem was a skinny kid, all rib cage. He palmed his crotch, looked out at his mother, still cinched in Old Gold's arms.

"Up!" said Heinrich.

They lifted the boy by the elbows, slid his feet into rawhide straps, tied his wrists down near the wheels. Lem swung there for a bit and Heinrich stooped to the floor, ran his fingers in the boy's hair.

"People," said Heinrich, "it is only through a symbolic reenactment of our deepest secret, our darkest desire, our most monumental shame, that we can ever hope to transcend our own limitude. Now look at this kid. Fucking incorrigible. Breaks all the rules. Steals food from the kitchen. Sneaks into town without permission. Brings back controlled goodies with which to obviate himself in the trance pasture. Well, boys will be boys. But boys will also someday be men. Childish men. Narcissistic sheep. In young Lem's case, however, we have an opportunity to avoid all that. He was just a small child when his mother brought him here, and let me tell you, our beloved Estelle was in pretty sad shape. A tumor with shoes, you want to know the truth. But she found the strength to heal herself, my friends. Her body saved, she sought then to be truly non-denominationally redeemed. Young Lem, it was decided, would be raised here among us. But though he began in purity the boy has become much corrupted over time. Good as dead, really. What are we to do? How do we effect some sort of reversal? We must try, at any rate. He belongs to all of us, in a way, but he still belongs to his mother most of all. And it is she who must save him now."

"No!" said Lem.

"Saw!" said Heinrich.

Naperton and another man slipped the hideous thing off its hooks, slid it down into the crack of the boy.

"Bad wiper," Naperton mouthed to the crowd.

"Now," said Heinrich, "when I say symbolic I don't mean that something very real isn't going to happen in a moment. Here's the deal: we're going to saw this little shitbird right the fuck in half unless his mommy sucks him off to big jiz. Big jiz! Them's the rules. I think fifteen minutes is fair. I mean, she's a mighty handsome woman. So, what do you all think? Pretty nifty, right? Lem, I figure you get through this, what in the whole wide fucking world is there left to fear? Rest easy, kid, in a little while you'll either be dead or a god. I only wish someone had done this for me. Estelle, my sweet, come on down!"

Old Gold wrestled the woman towards her son. Benches scraped the floor and tipped. Brethren scurried, parted.

I stood, shook Trubate's hand off my arm.

"This is fucking crazy!" I shouted. "Stop this now! Take him down!"

"Or what?"

"I'll call the police. They might be interested in your idea of dinner theater."

"Steve," said Heinrich, "darling Steve, that there is the threat of a victim, not a hero. A phone call? You're going to make a phone call? Man, are you neck deep in the big dark darkety dark."

"Take him down now," I said.

I saw heavy movement in my periphery. Heinrich bore down on me with glittery eyes.

"Hey," he said. "It's just a hummer."

Items #4

Heinrich said, "Start anywhere."

Heinrich said, "Let memory scamper to the glades of the now."

It's hard to believe people buy this brand of tripe. But then you picture the very same man pressing a SIG Sauer barrel to the brow of a sleeping Indian, a trussed nun.

You let it slide.

Heinrich gave me a ballpoint pen, a notebook with a Velcro flap. The Velcro, he said, was so I'd feel safe.

"Like a seat belt?" I said.

It was a good pop, spleen region. Put me on my knees.

"Like a seat belt," he said. "That's humorous."

It's hard to know what's humorous anymore.

I started the first notebook soon after my head wound healed, the one I received the night Estelle Burke publicly pleasured her son. Sorry to say I missed that particular spectacle. It was Parish, I later discovered, who did me my concussive honors, employing what he termed the "old cast-iron hat."

I've been writing, or itemizing, as they call it, ever since.

Heinrich says I'd better get it all down. He believes I'm really dying. Sees it in my eyes, he says. Dimness and some flickering. It's nothing any doctor could detect.

"What if I'm not dying?" I say.

"God forbid," he says.

"Itemize, itemize," he says.

I haven't written anything like this in years. The copy I confected for a living was never more than a line or two, designed to capture the allure of the new, to shimmer with efficient leisure and sumptuous toil, the ongoing orgasm of the information lifestyle: "Software with a Soft Touch," I wrote, or "Reality for Those Who Dream," or, simply, "How Did You Like Tomorrow?"

You've probably seen my work on billboards, on takeout coffee cups, between perfumed pullouts in those surveys of venality otherwise known as slicks. Somebody actually wrote this crap, you said to yourself.

You were absolutely right.

I was a droplet in the steady rain of crap.

I had, I guess, like my father before me, a naïf's faith in words. When I was twelve, thirteen, I won the fire safety essay contest for a longish tract, "The Oil-Soaked Rags of Death."

Captain Thornfield, he of the silvery sidewhiskers and exquisitely braided dress cap, lauded my genius to an assembly of my peers.

"You boys and girls should take some pointers from this young man," said the captain. "Most especially the part about how the family unit must establish a regrouping area a good distance from any hypothetical conflagration."

I took his praise to be the seeds of fervent tutelage. The next contest nearly a year away, I dashed off another treatise, "Five Alarm Soul: Studies in Hazard," delivered it to the captain at the borough fire station. Included was an appendix citing each instance of tire tower thuggery I'd suffered at the hands of his hoodlum sons. I wanted the poor man to forsake his blood for the purity of our flame-retardant enterprise, to rid himself of his progeny, take me under his sooty wing.

I never heard back from the captain.

Then it was all those English major essays, user manuals for the spirit's vaporware.

I was kind of a whiz at it, too. My father took pride in my hermeneutic seizuring. He wanted for his son anything but his mode, a poetics in the service of multispeed blenders. I shamed him soon enough, shilling for the silicon sultanates.

"Too Much? Too Fast? Tough Cookies—Deal or Die," I wrote when they wanted something Boom-punchy.

I got a raise, an options package, new digs.

I got a regrouping area in hell.

It'd be nice to know how long I've been here at the Center. Clocks and calendars do not abound. Heinrich says he won't turn tricks for time, that suns and moons and seasons are taunts enough. Sometimes I crave the old exactitude, daydream about the timepieces I threw away back when the Philosopher and the Mechanic first handed down my verdict, my suspended sentence, my frozen state. Now I live life in vague thick drift, my days something crated in Styrofoam, shipment on hold.

I got a phone privilege a while back, called Fiona, begged her to fetch me, her suffering pa. She said she was locked into her own emotional arc at the moment, couldn't afford the shift in trajectory.

She'll be fourteen in June.

"Besides, Daddy," she said. "What are you complaining about? You're alive, aren't you? You're riddled with PREXIS and you're defying all odds. Something must be working."

"I'm not riddled. I hate that. Riddled. Anyway, there's probably no such thing as PREXIS."

"Whatever, dude. I mean, Dad."

Every morning after First Calling I do my bubble dance while Parish preps, a vegetable slaughter. The man raves on between swipes of his Chinese cleaver.

"You're in the weeds now, skipper! You're in the weedy weeds! Look at all those spoons and saucers! They're so dirty!"

"I'm a crawling king snake," I say.

"You're nothing, babyducks. I'm the stewman and you're the stewboy. I'm your daddy in food!"

"Knock it off, Parish."

Which only induces him to start thwapping me with a slotted spoon.

"Baby! Babycakes!"

"Cut the shit, Parish."

"I'll cut your mother's shit. I'll eat it."

"Bet you will."

"Is that an insult?"

"Just let me do my job."

"You don't have a job, you have a chore. Read the fucking *Tenets*."

"I've read them."

"All you've read is the back of the tater tot box."

Thwap.

"Stop it."

"I'll stop when you admit to me that I'm the stewman and you're the stewboy."

"Okay, Parish, I'm the stewboy. But you're crazy."

"I'm in a healing process, yuppie fuck. I walk the high road."

Thwap.

"Violence will be met with decisive violence," I say.

"Very good. You *have* read the *Tenets*. That's a nice one, too. I'll make sure it's engraved on your tombstone, Skippy."

Thwap. Thwap.

Punch bread time, perchance?

Emancipated by the advent of Parish's inevitable dopamine downtick, I'll seek solitude in the trance pasture, or study the *Tenets* until dinnertime. Some nights Heinrich might have a word or two for the collective ear, a disquisition on the condition of our republic, the United Stooges of Moronica, he calls it, or, rarely, announce an evening of cabin visits. There's a weekly square dance called by Parish which enough of us boycott to render the event more amplified cris de coeur than hoedown. ("Bow to your partner," Parish will command, "now bow to your neighbor who was banging your partner while you were in the hospital with hepatitis.")

Mostly I look for lulls in the evening when I can slip off to the brush with Renee. Yes, Renee. Her initial bluff was hurt entreaty, I guess, because a few mornings after we met she wheeled up to my cabin door and announced she was curious about terminal cock.

"Seduction is a subtle art," I said.

"I'm not seducing you," said Renee. "This is a field study."

Now I'm always scouting for a clearing to which to wheel my voluptuous crip. Nippy nights are a hardship but I pack a quilt and we make our rough way up the hill trail towards the ever-so-mysterious mothering hut. Sometimes we ditch the chair and I bear her in a fireman's carry—look at me, Captain Thornfield!—over the roots and crags, lower us down behind some cold oak. Compensation is not the word for what Renee does with her hands and her mouth to triumph over her dead half. I've discovered marooned colonies of feeling down there, too. We'll lie under moonlight for hours, tell jokes, sing jingles, make puppets of our private parts. I'll kiss her breasts, kiss the blue vein in one of them that must flow to her heart, a quiet river running through a church.

Speaking of church, it was organized religion that stole my baby's legs away. Some soused bishop jumped a curbside in his El Camino. This was in her hometown, Neptune, New Jersey. Renee was just seventeen, window-shopping for a slutty top for school. She spent a year in bed and a few more trying to be a miracle of physical therapy, dreamed of the day she'd stagger through a cheering gauntlet of male nurse beefcake, but she never got past cod flops on the padded floor. She took to gin, launched a newsletter called *Gimp Snatch*. Heinrich found her doing wheelchair doughnuts in the parking lot of Arman's Adult Motel. He told her he was trolling for souls. She said she'd blow him for a ride home. That was years and years ago.

She says she's humped most everyone here except Parish and DaShawn, whose goiter and imperious manner drove her away. She says she'll do who she pleases, that no God or blitzed minion of Him, or, for that matter, any kind of cut-rate chariot will stop her from being the woman that girl on the sidewalk was outfitting herself to become.

I do worship her mostly paralyzed pussy and I am maybe in love.

She says she admires my hands, so ladylike.

I told her I'd let that slide.

"Of course you will," she said. "You're my lady."

This morning Naperton took the van down to the city to hawk our redemptive hoop at the farmer's market. I've shopped there myself in a former life, strolled rows of kiosks manned by suspicious Amish with their Lincoln beards and judgmental scones, tarried at fruit bins and herb trays tended by Wall Street dropouts, or runaway teens with tracts on bio-dynamism in their rucksacks.

Oversoul Spread, I understand, is big with the Sunday gourmands. There's a mail-order business, too. Sales, along with exhaustive donations from the Center's more moneyed brethren, keep us in Parish's improvisatory slops while we mother and trance ourselves to redemption. Only those with exorbitant levels of continuum awareness are permitted to make the trip. A cheese run is high honor.

We eat gobs of the stuff, too. It spreads thin, tastes a bit like a battery.

"It's what the city people crave, Skippo," Parish said. "They think the cheese will cleanse them of their sins. They're not about to be mothered by fire now, are they?"

"Are you?"

"I've been in the hut. I'll be in it again. I'll get it right."

Parish was a line cook in a Chapel Hill ribhouse until the day a customer died on his shift.

"So I put peanut butter in the chili. So what? It's a time-honored thickener. One in a million the bitch would be allergic, and her old man a goddamn state senator, to boot. There's a law named for her now. Ever hear of LuAnn's Law? It's a food safety bill. It's an anti-peanut-butter bill, really. Which, if you look at it historically, the peanut and its uses being the achievement of a black scientist, that would make LuAnn's Law a piece of racist legislation, ask me. But nobody does ask me. Nobody ever asks me. At least to cook for a living. Not anymore. Who'll hire the big bad chili killer? That's when it all started for me. Smack, whiskey, alimony, syph."

"Sounds like a song."

"Oh, it's a song all right. Now get on the stick, Stewboy. Papa's got a brand-new spatula. Spanky-spanky."

Funny how even the nutters get sane enough for the few minutes it takes to spill their guts.

Then it's the redeye back to Batshit Isle.

Today I sat in the trance pasture for a good hour after First Calling. I shut my eyes and made to enter that peaceful ripple of a kingdom Heinrich calls the shit-free zone. It was a nice place to visit until that wife-filcher William started bum-rushing my void.

Scamper, scamper.

I met William in the dorm rooms of higher yearning. He'd wormed a double for himself down the hall, a sumptuous bong chamber tricked out with batiks by spree killers and oil portraits of famous French Marxists he'd painted on black velvet. He fancied himself some kind of conceptualist at the time. Everything was a concept. Every concept was ripe for dismemberment. He liked to trace punk rock back to the age of Luther, don used toupees.

I once asked him who the hell he thought he was.

"A gangster of contingency," he explained.

He was my hero and for my worship I got first dibs on the women he'd bed and flee. My job, as I saw it, was to coddle them back to some sort of flummoxed spite, whereupon they'd jerk me around for a while, the William proxy, then give me the boot.

I thought it a commendable system at the time.

Someday William and his cruel, pretty face would be known to all the world, of that I was also convinced. Artist, philosopher, provocateur, such petty designations would merely constrict his force. I figured I'd best tag along and witness this bloom, be his blasted Boswell: *Behind the Scenes with William P; William P: A Life, an Art; The Pucked Bowl: The Life and Times of William P.*

Other fevers seized him, though.

Next thing, William's scoring callbacks from the leading investment firms in the country.

"Dudes are making scads," he told me, chopping down some crystal on a Baader-Meinhof pop-up book.

He'd taken to wearing twills.

"What happened to contingency?" I said.

"What could be more contingent than money?"

He looked almost priestly there at the snort end of his soda straw.

Make no mistake, I was happy to see him when I spotted him years later thumbing violently through Peruvian flute disks at a midtown megastore. He was a tad pastier now, pinched into some flashy tailoring, maybe a Milanese number. I noticed a kind of bleary epiphany in his eyes when he saw me, as though I were some object mislaid long ago with not a little remorse.

I kissed him, called him Billy, took him home to meet the family.

File it under fuckup, I guess. Warm and defeated as he'd seemed in the megastore, William came to merciless life over linguine and wine. Maryse was in his thrall well before the garlic loaf was out of the oven, and there was Fiona at the far end of the table, making nervous pokes at her head hole.

Poor dear, poor daughter, torn between deadbeat biology and this glad shimmer of a man. William was rich, toothy, world-luminous. He had tales to tell, wisdom to dispense. I was bitter and middling and whatever I dispensed tended to stain my shorts.

It was never much of a contest.

"You're shaking," somebody said.

DaShawn stood over me here in the trance pasture. His tunic was soiled. His goiter looked bigger.

"Shaking with solitude," I said.

"Sorry, then. I was wrong to disturb you."

"How's the merc trade? Kill any Continentals today?"

"Whoa," said DaShawn. "Let's get something straight here. I'm not some nutbin Napoleon. I know who I am and, more importantly, *when* I am. I have a degree in indigenous studies from Ramapo State College. I just prefer traditional dress."

"I'm sorry, DaShawn. You have to understand that I'm an asshole."

"I do understand."

I started to thank the man for such rare comprehension.

"Shhh. I want to show you something."

DaShawn led me out of the pasture and through some brush. We hiked our way up the hill trail through a steep rise of spruce.

"What are you doing?" I said.

"I told you, I want to show you something."

A burning scent was coming off the mountain, rich and dry, full of campfire cheer. We strayed off the trail and hacked our way up to a great forked elder. There in a clear was a tiny cottage built of thatch and brick. Smoke rifled out the tin flue.

"Ye Olde Mothering Hut," said DaShawn.

"I wonder who's in there," I said.

"Heinrich's in there. And somebody. We never know who it is until it's all over. That way there's no shame."

Now shrieks carried over the clear.

"Damn," I said.

"The Iroquois," said DaShawn, "in fact many of the eastern tribes, not to mention the plains tribes, prided themselves on their ability to bear torture. If you got captured by an enemy, you were already dead and disgraced. Your only recourse was to maintain dignity during the ordeal."

"Stoic."

"Not stoic. They'd go bananas. You motherfucking bear-fucker, your tribe is rabbit shit. Something to say while you're being flensed alive."

"Was this passed down in family lore, DaShawn?"

"I researched it for my thesis. My family passed down a fondness for Ring-Dings."

"We had Devil Dogs," I said.

"Those are good, too."

A man stooped out of the hut. Bits of ash hung in the air about him. He was naked, smeared with soot and blood. A piece of metal poked out of his hand.

We saw a flash, heard a boom, felt something thud into the elder.

Tonight, after pears in syrup, Heinrich stood for a word. He'd showered, looked rested, his wet hair combed back into an impromptu pompadour. There were still a few streaks of ash on his hands, a little scallop of dried blood on his ear.

"People, I have an announcement to make. It concerns our very own Bobby Trubate. Today was an extra-special day for him. You know of what I speak. It's uncertain if we'll ever see him again, but suffice it to say he has finally tasted truth. Trubate. Perhaps name is destiny, after all."

"You hear that, Spanky?" Parish whispered into my ear.

I nodded, spooned up some pear.

Back at the cabin Old Gold was stuffing Bobby's clothes into a duffel bag.

"Did he go home?"

"I don't know," said Old Gold.

"What happened?"

"I don't know. I guess he was no match for mothering fire."

"He's a good guy."

"Avram, has it ever occurred to you that a lot of this stuff might be figurative? That really the idea of life is just to get along as best we can under the circumstances?"

"Oh, you mean like Nazi Germany?"

"Don't pull that Nazi shit with me. I'm a Jew, too."

"Who said I was a Jew?"

"I read it in your story in the *Tenets*."

"Maybe I just meant that figurative."

Old Gold left and I lay in my cot for a while. My classical kindergarten education had trained me to always take a few moments before sleep to review my day, ruminate on any schoolyard atrocities the banality of evil or banality may have glossed. Pigtail tuggings. Marble-maimings. Bastard shot at me, was all I could think. My day, for the most part. There was a knock at the door and Heinrich capered in all soft-shoe, twirled a phantom baton.

"Cabin visit."

"Are you going to tuck me in?"

"I could, but then you'd just get up again to proceed with your wheelchair assignations."

"No secrets around here, huh?"

"Renee," said Heinrich. "Poor kid came here thinking about miracles. Just like you. People get crazy ideas. Even smart people like Renee. They think they're going to overcome their personal tragedies. They employ the phrase 'personal tragedy.' But I have deep feeling for Renee, I do. Marooned colonies of feeling, even."

"No respect for Velcro, either."

"Privacy's a dead end, Steve. What's the saying? Last refuge of scumbags?"

"Do you read everyone's items?"

"I paid for the pen, man. And the paper. So, how did you like being shot at today?"

"Is that what that was?"

"Toughie. How's your mysterious rot going?"

"I'm not sure."

"That's a good sign."

"The symptoms come and go."

"As they will."

"It's not all in my head."

"Hey, if it's in your head it's in you."

"I'll try to remember that," I said. "Or my head will. What were you doing to Trubate in the mothering hut?"

"Midwifery."

"What happened?"

"You were there."

"Is he dead?"

"Why would he be dead?"

"Because his things were still here. Because I heard those screams. Because you—"

"Careful now. I what?"

"I don't know."

"No, you don't, do you? You're deducing again."

"I want to leave here."

"And go where?"

"Home."

"Where would that be?"

"Shit," I said, "you tell me."

I threw a fit. I decided to throw a fit. It was a technique I'd honed at the agency. Sometimes, uncertain times, it proved judicious to appear unhinged. A timely spaz bespoke passion, salary-worth. Mine were maybe tantamount to office culture, too, like the late-night car service or the Monday massage. Don't pitch a Steve, people would admonish, except they said something else because as I may have mentioned, my name isn't Steve. Now I careened around the cabin looking for props. Swipes and kicks were a crucial part of the show. I started for the Coleman, dreaming of a drywood blaze. Heinrich stuck his foot out. There was time to clear it but I tripped anyway. The finish is the hardest part of the fit. That foot was a gift.

"Calm yourself," said Heinrich.

"Thank you," I said.

"Are you calm?"

"Extremely fucking calm."

Heinrich put his hand out.

"Listen," he said. "This is your home. You have to accept that fact. Acceptance is the key to everything. I need you to be the hero of your own life, Steve. Also, I need your help."

"My help."

"Work for me, son. Don't be embarrassed. The dependence of a great man upon a greater is a subjection that lower men cannot easily comprehend."

"Who said that?"

"Halifax."

"I wouldn't know him."

"I read his maxims on the can. The cheese spread has real possibilities. We need some snap. We need some pop. Soft cheese for a soft touch."

"Now you're quoting me quoting myself."

"Too heavy for me," said Heinrich. "The levels, the levels. But I know you'll do us proud. One more thing. Don't ever sneak up on me at the hut again. I'll put one in your neck. Now, let me see your eyes. That's what I thought."

"What?"

"More dimness. Less flickering."

The ant trundling a piece of thread across my windowsill had a brain punier than the blackhead I was teasing out of my nose with opposed thumbnails, but he must dream, mustn't he? Of what? Love? Work? Popcorn skins? Bolts of lint? Maze rats dreamed of mazes, according to the latest studies. Maze rat scientists dreamed of rats. I was dreaming of cheese.

I scoured my corporate memory for all those phrases we used to bat around in lieu of competence. Brand leverage, brand agility, viral replication of the core brand identity. How about isotopic marketing? Meme buzz? Meme juice? Brand spill? The older types, the so-called salesmen, they'd laugh at us, go on about how there was no difference between hawking a webcasting network and an oatmeal cookie. Then they'd beg us for cocaine. Me, I was never much of a salesman. Sometimes, in my cups, or in a moment of weak arrogance, I called myself a court poet in the multinational kingdom. Better days I'd just call myself a hack and get on with the work.

Renee lay beside me in my cot, the *Tenets* tilted on her belly.

"Don't pop it," she said.

"Why not?"

"I want to."

I tendered my nose to the lamplight.

"Go ahead."

"Hey," said Renee, "did you know Heinrich has a son? Or had a son?"

"It says that in the book? I missed it. Ow!"

"There," said Renee, held out the dark squiggle, my coagulated essence, in her palm. "It's vague, towards the end of the preface: 'My only issue emerged somewhat amphibious, due to pharmaceutical miscalculation on the part of his mother. He lived for a while in a ventilated, see-through tube. Then he returned to precellular nullity.' "

"That's not so vague. How could I have missed that?"

"I think I have an older edition."

"Why would he take it out?"

"Why would he put it in?" said Renee. "At least like that?"

"That's part of his appeal."

"Appeals to you, maybe."

"What aspect of the master most pleases you, young novice?"

"His shoulders. From behind he looks like my father."

"Women and their fathers," I said.

"Is that supposed to be insightful?"

"It's a saying," I said.

"You have a daughter, don't you?"

"I did. I definitely did."

"You're breaking my heart. I feel my heart actually cleaving. Is cleaving the word?"

"We thought the school was a good idea."

"I'm sure it was. It's you and your wife that weren't such a good idea."

"We tried."

"That's what I mean."

"Lay off, okay? I want to ask you something. Did you know Heinrich reads our item books?"

"We give them to him. Before we're mothered by fire."

"I mean all the time."

"I don't think so."

"He read mine."

"He must like you."

"I don't trust the bastard."

"Don't talk that way, Steve."

"I'm not Steve."

"You keep saying that. I'm all for mantras, but really, the trick is to find one that isn't so rooted in negation."

"Listen, why don't you drag your numb ass back into your little fucking go-cart and get lost. I have work to do."

The compound was quiet tonight, lit low by a pale slice of moon in the sky. The wind carried moans of milk cows in their stalls. Renee wheeled off near the dining-hall door without a word. She'd been crying. I'd thought she'd been sneezing but she told me through snot-wet bursts that this was how she cried. Wires crossed up after the accident. Not that I would care. Now I looked over towards Heinrich's cabin. He sat near the window, reading by candlelight. Strains of some cantata poured through the crevices of his home. His sloped shoulders bucked with what looked to be spasms of amusement. Maybe

Renee's father laughed like that. I sneaked up to the sill. Let him put one in my neck, I thought.

Heinrich saw me, cracked his window.

"Evening," he said. "Out for a stroll?"

He laid the pamphlet he was reading on the sill. *Adult Children of War Criminals: A Copebook.*

"Cheese to Ease the Disease," I said.

"Not bad," said Heinrich.

"It's terrible," I said.

"Yes," said Heinrich, "it is."

"I don't have to help you, you know."

"It's a free country. A dry county, but a free country."

"I don't even know what the hell I'm doing here. I think it's some bizarre belief that the more ridiculous the situation is, the better the chances of something good coming from it."

"That is bizarre," said Heinrich.

"You don't have the fucking cure," I said.

"Good night, Steve."

"You know, you could go to prison for what you're doing here."

"I could go to prison for lots of stuff," said Heinrich.

Dietz called me over from his doorway. He said he had some bourbon, a little weed. Lem was building a customer base. Dietz's cabin was small and stank of Dietz. Books and torn parts of books and chunks of cinder littered the floor. There was a doorless mini-fridge in the corner. Pasted over the opening was a poster of a well-stocked ice box—pickle jars, milk jugs, wrapped steaks, fruit. Dietz sat on a steamer trunk with his derby in his lap. He was pinching out the creases in the brim. His Coleman threw light up on his berry stain. He caught me staring at it.

"Mark of Cain," he said. "Born with the thing."

"I like it."

"I don't care so much about it. When I was a kid, sure. Girls, before I met the right kind. But it's hard to get people to look you in the eye. Look me in the eye."

"I'm looking."

"Yes, you are."

"What do you want, Dietz?"

"What do I want? What a question. I remember when I was a child my folks took me out to the beach. I hadn't said a word yet. Mute little fucker. Far back on the baby curve. But it so happened that on that day I saw something out on the water. Something that appealed to me. It appealed to me enough to summon language in me. Language was called up from my tiny toddler database for the first time in my tiny miserable life. What do you think I said? Remember, I saw something that appealed to me."

"Seagull," I said. "See the seagull."

"That would be grand, Steve. See the seagull. I'd be a fucking poet now, wouldn't I? No, I did not say see the seagull. What I said was, I want boat. That's all I said. I want boat."

"You knew what you wanted."

"My mother was amazed. She cried, she says. She says she cried."

"Did you get boat?"

"They took me out on a day cruise. Bought tickets, bundled me up. They were not wealthy people, Steve. Vermont syrup trash, tell the truth. But, like I said, they bought tickets, bundled me up, walked me up the gangway. We're out five minutes and I'm a goddamn disaster area. Or so I've been told. Five minutes sounds like an exaggeration, an embolism, not an embolism, you know what I mean."

"An embellishment."

"Point is, I'm a wreck. Puking, weeping. Sea sickness. The sickness of the fucking sea. And it's at this moment in the experience I make utterance once more. Once more language is called upon to do my bidding. What do you think I said?"

"There are so many possibilities."

"No, there aren't. You're missing it. Think about it logically. What could I have said? Okay, I'll tell you what I said. No more boat. That's what I said. No more boat. Now, I'm a dude, I'm the kind of dude that can babble on and on. To anybody. About anything. How many times, for instance, do you think I've said a word like anybody, or anything, in my life? Millions, probably. How many times have I said the word probably? How many times have I used my gift of language to explicate myself out of this or that shit-fucked situation?"

"Extricate."

"How many times have I said shit-fucked, or situation? Brother, it's all language. Dope, cars, finger-banging, rock 'n' roll. It's all just language. You think it's not, buddy, but it is, trust me. You think the ultimate is out there somewhere, beyond language, but it's not. It's just totally not. For example, what's the ultimate, anyway? It's a fucking word. But here's my final point, Steve. For all those goddamn words, for all those combinatory combinations of words, for all their various shades and schadenfreudes of meaning or unmeaning, it just comes down to two basic things. I want boat and no more boat. That's all there is."

"I know what you mean."

"You have no idea what I mean. Do you really like my stain? Or do you mean to say you like to look at it?"

"What's the difference?" I said.

"That's a good question. I wish I had the answer. But I'm just a dumbfuck. I'm just trying to keep it together."

"Did you know Wendell?"

"I knew Wendell."

"What happened to him?"

"He couldn't find the language," said Dietz. "Hungry?"

He pointed to his picture of food.

Bobby Trubate was back in his cot, hooked to a drip, wrapped in loose gauze. His face was bruised and runny, his mustache singed down to a ridge of hairy blisters. He looked like some formerly majestic bird pulled from a crash site fuselage.

"Jesus, Bobby," I said. "What'd he do to you?"

"Saved me," said Trubate.

Estelle lounged in the corner with a magazine from the Johnson administration. There were stacks of these around, good for pop scholarship, kindling. I don't know who collected them, but paeans to the sexual revolution and tawny sideburns abounded. I tended to pore over the ads myself, stereos like space bays, secret sodomy in the Rob Roy ice.

"Funny to read this crap, now," she said. "It's like inscriptions in your yearbook. Remember me when you're a movie star. Send me a postcard from Paris."

"We need to get him to a hospital."

"He'll be fine. I've been looking after him."

"They took his stuff."

"There's a laundry run."

Trubate began to moan. His body sputtered under the sheets.

"Did you know," said Estelle, "that before this was the Center for Nondenominational Recovery and Redemption, it was a POW camp?"

"A what?"

"Simulated. For executive types. They'd come up here for a huge fee and Heinrich would keep them in cages, torture them."

"Didn't read that part in the *Tenets*."

"Editorial discretion."

It looked like Bobby wanted to speak. His lips split their scab caulk and sound dribbled out.

"Maa . . . Faa . . ."

"Ma?"

"What is it?" said Estelle.

"Maah . . . Faah . . ."

"Mother," I said. "Father."

"No," said Estelle. "Mothered by Fire. He's acknowledging his passage."

"Maah . . ."

"What is it, Bobby?" I said.

Trubate strained up from the bed.

"My face," he said. "My fucking face."

Estelle was tired. I told her I'd watch Trubate for a while. He slept like a stone, or a stoned man. Maybe there was some morphine in his drip. His wounds, I saw now, were mostly superficial, show-biz gashes. Character-building for the character actor. Maybe he could ride the crest of the next disfigurement fad to stardom.

Me, I was going to ride the hell out of here. There was nothing for me here, nothing shit-free. Organized psychosis had its rewards, but I was pretty sure you needed a future to reap them. I was a dying man, futureless. A lone wolf. A lone wraith.

I dozed at Trubate's bedside, got up near dawn, walked back to Heinrich's window. He was asleep at his desk when I tapped on the pane. Heinrich didn't wake so much as boot up. You could almost sense the circuits firing, the cautious ascent to speed.

"I need to talk to you," I said.

"Your need is your demand," said Heinrich, waved me in.

We sat in wicker, sipped root tea. Books, bales of them—paperbacks, hardbacks, chapbooks, manuals, sheaves—spilled out the rough pine shelves. There were survival guides and bird guides and bound sets of American Transcendentalists, but also computer manuals and some simulation theory I recalled my pal William flogging himself to ecstatic bongstates with in college. Heinrich set his tea mug down on an upturned clementine crate. He followed my gaze to the encrusted Esperanto phrasebook beside it.

"Since the misfortune in Babel it has been a dream," he said. "I think it's folly, myself. Everyone should sing his own incomprehensible, inconsolable song. What I want to do here is help people find it."

"Is that why you ran a POW camp?" I said.

"That was a business proposition."

"Clearly not a very lucrative one."

"I did okay. Look, Steve, I'm a soldier. I've been all over the world hurting people. I don't apologize. Who am I to apologize? But this, all of this, it's a surprise to me. What I . . . what *we* have done here. What we've made. You've heard me make my crazy speeches to them. My beast-tales. Maybe I have fuck's clue what I'm talking about, but at least I am talking. And maybe we're getting somewhere, too. The mothering hut. Who could have known the power of such a thing? It just came to me one day. I thought it was an interrogation facility. It *was* an interrogation facility. We used it for a sweat lodge in the off-season. Naperton said it first. Like giving birth to yourself in there."

"Sounds like kitchen duty."

"Hardly."

"I guess I'll have to ask Dobby about that."

"Mister Fucking Melodrama. You love this stuff, don't you? You loved it when those quacks told you you were dying and you love thinking I have some awful plan for you. And here I was banking on the idea that your cowardice was just a surface ploy. You really are addicted to your existence, aren't you? You'd be better off strung out on smack."

"I just came to say goodbye."

"Goodbye."

"And thank you."

"For what?"

"I don't know."

"There's going to be a reckoning tonight. Old Gold will face his demon. I think you should stick around. Maybe you'll change your mind about all of this. If you don't, wait outside your cabin. Naperton's making a cheese run tonight. He'll give you a ride."

"I'll be there."

"It's too bad," said Heinrich.

"What's that?"

"I was hoping you'd be my entrée into a whole new market."

"I'll recommend you at the racquet club."

I did the day. I did the rest of the day. I went to the kitchen for my bubble dance. I did big hellos.

"What are you grinning about?" said Parish.

"These all the dishes?" I said. "Bring it on! Greasy platters, gunked spoons, the dried ketchup of martyrs! Bring the shit on, Parish! I am the cleanser."

"Who gave you permission for giddiness, you little shit? Listen, I'm in a funk. I'm in no mood."

"I'm all moods," I said. "In and out of them."

"I'm the boss of you," said Parish. "I set the mood."

We squared off. I got up on boxer's toes, popped Parish in the tit. He dropped me with a whisk handle to the mouth. I got up, got quiet, rubbed my teeth.

"Oh, don't be sulky," said Parish. "I think you're charming. I'm just having a day. Too many peepers on the potatoes. I don't like to be so seen by tubers. I'm sorry. You're the cleanser, okay?"

"I'm the cleanser," I said.

"That's my boy. Now don't forget to punch out."

My rye'd gone green.

I went back to the cabin to check on Trubate. The room was dark and stank of balm. He was sitting up, the drip ripped from his arm. He stared up at the rafter beam.

"Bobby?" I said.

"Bobby died in a fire," he said.

I walked out to the trance pasture, saw Lem Burke sitting in the punk weeds, smoking a joint, gerrymandering an ant colony with a stick.

"Got some of those in my cabin," I said.

"What?"

"Ants."

"What kind of ants?"

"I don't know. Black ants."

"These are red ants."

"Communists."

"I wouldn't say that," said Lem. "They just do what seems right."

Lem whipped the stick. It careened off my knee.

"Sorry," he said.

The weeds were high. I could only make out the top of the kid's head. He was so long and scrawny, weedlike himself. It seemed like he'd always been here, sitting, dreaming, playing Hitler with dirt life.

"Hear about Old Gold?" I said.

"Poor fucker," said Lem.

"You don't like it here, do you?"

Lem said nothing.

"How's your continuum awareness coming?"

"Why do you ask so many questions?" said Lem. "What are you trying to hide?"

"Sometimes people ask questions just to find out things."

"My continuum awareness is coming along fine," said Lem. "The past present and future are entirely saturated with one thought, one image, one sensation. My mom knew what she was doing, tell you that."

Smoke was rolling off the ridge. Both of us sniffed at the sky. Wolves, I thought. Rabbits, I revised.

"That man Wendell who had my cabin," I said. "What happened to him?"

"He died."

"Heinrich says he hanged himself."

"You know you splooge in your pants when you do that?"

"Yeah," I said.

"Guess everyone knows. I'm finding that the older I get, it's not that I learn new things, it's more like I find out how much of what I know is common knowledge."

"That's a good way of putting it."

"Don't condescend."

"I'm not."

"Don't deny your actions."

Lem was truly a child of this place.

"Did Wendell leave a note? An explanation?"

"Yeah. There was a note. It said, Please note."

"Please note?"

"Please note."

"Damn," I said.

"That's what I said. Want some of this?"

"Yes," I said.

I hardly noticed Lem leave. I hardly noticed anything except the helium panic of the pot, the warp of the world, the fissuring. I decided to give the shit-free zone one more shot. No more boat. No more no-more-boat. I thought about nothing. I zeroed in on nothingness. Nothingness rose out of the ether to greet me, to embrace. I heard music now, horns, a brassy vamp. Flashpots, fireworks. The nothingness dancers chorus-kicked through smoke.

"Please note! Please note!" they sang. Kick-turn. Kick-turn. Balcony gels, leotards, hip jut. This was not for nothing, I thought. Then the weed wore off. The garter belts fell from the trees. The sun was going down.

I did not hate twilight.

I went to fetch Renee.

I rolled her out to the milk barn to see the calf twins born last week. Romulus and Rimjob, Old Gold had named them. They were dark and frisky in the moonlit pen, big sweet pups. They nuzzled our knees at the rail. Renee put her hand out and one of them took it with a soft sucking sound up to the wrist.

"Oh, my God," she said.

"I'm sorry," I said, "about those things I said the other night."

"You have to try this," said Renee.

"I need to tell you something," I said.

"You really have to try this."

I stuck a loose fist out for the other calf. It made a rough warm womb of its mouth for me.

"Jesus," I said. "That really is something."

"Isn't it? No wonder cows are sacred in Japan."

"I don't think it's Japan," I said.

"I hate you," said Renee. "Let's have a hate fuck."

"Over there, then," I said, "behind the hayrick."

"That's called a hayrick?" said Renee.

"Sure," I said.

"Sounds like Heinrich," said Renee.

"Don't say that," I said.

There were no dessert speeches that night. We bused our plates and marched out of the dining hall. Portable lights lit the lawn outside, night-game bright. There was a chop in the air and the lamp casings hummed. Somewhere behind us an engine gunned. The glow of brake lights parted us.

Naperton slid down from the van, popped the hatch, reached in to struggle with some kind of ungainly parcel. The thing seemed to twitch in its plummet and when it hit the lawn we saw what it was—a man. He wore a blindfold, handcuffs of clear plastic. Blood had dried on his shaven head. Naperton pulled the blindfold off. The man just stood there and blinked for a while. The lights were probably putting a wildness in his eyes but he looked a tad touched anyway, the type who spends his childhood plucking butterflies apart, or Scotch-taping patriotic ordnance to gerbils, only to make his way up the living chain in a great pageant of abuse.

But who am I to talk, mastermind of the Moth-O-Caust?

He had tattoos. A steely anchor on his sternum tipped into a fat black heart. A target spiraled out from the top of his skull. The bull's-eye read "C.B." There was a logo on his shoulder that looked familiar. I nearly retched when I read the legend beneath it: *Tough Cookies—Deal or Die*.

Now we all watched as Clellon Beach rolled to his knees and made to somehow stand.

Naperton kicked him in the hip.

"Fuck you," said Beach.

"Fuck me?" said Naperton. "I'm old enough to be your grandfather. You wouldn't want to fuck me."

Naperton kicked him in the mouth. Tooth bits stuck to Beach's lip.

"That all you got?" he said.

"For now," said Naperton. "Try our sales representative tomorrow. Unless you'd be interested in this."

Naperton kicked him in the stomach. Beach puked through his teeth.

"Picador," said Heinrich from the porch, "I think the bull is ready."

He stood at the balustrade in a stained dinner jacket and a wire-fastened beard, Odin emceeing a varsity football banquet.

"Dig the beard?" he said. "Had the thing in my closet for years. I was God one Halloween, if you can believe it. Costume contest. Some Little Orphan Annie cunt won. Mr. Beach, it's an honor to finally meet you. You're a storied figure in our later gospels, so it really is a privilege. 'A huge fucking killer,' if I remember the text correctly. Well, maybe not so huge. What do you go, one-forty, one forty-five? But then again, Abraham didn't live hundreds of years, either, did he? Mythology is beyond fact-checking, I'd say. Wouldn't you? Did they tell you why you're here?"

The man moaned.

"I didn't hear you," said Heinrich.

"I told them," said Beach. "There was nothing in the container, I swear. I went on board myself. It was empty."

"What container?"

"The container."

"All day," said Naperton, "about the container. The fore-deck container, he says."

"Thank you, Notty. I do believe I understand. Clellon, are you thinking you're here because of some dirtbag job you botched? Some double-cross you cooked up in a Norfolk flop-house? These are things of Clellon Beach the man. We don't give a rat's ass about him around here. We are solely concerned with myth. And you are myth, Mr. Beach. You are the demon who stalks our beloved Gold. Through no fault of your own, I might add. Nonetheless, now there must be a reckoning. Can we get some drum?"

Dietz walked out of the crowd doing paradiddles on a fur-bound Indian tom.

"This isn't a fucking Krupa show," said Heinrich. "Slow it down."

Now Old Gold stepped out to the porch, shirtless, in festive pantaloons. He gripped his terrific knife. Bobby was there, if he was still Bobby, pulped a bit around the eyes, the *Tenets* open in his hands and him nearly davening as he recited: "Behold, sub-sequent diagnostic procedures proved it so, and subsequent forays into the abyss revealed these things to me: Your soul is made of deeds. Your thoughts, your fears, your whims, your doubts, are sand. Moreover, you can't make an omelet without perpetrating some serious fucking atrocities. Mama, Papa, Caca, Pee-Pee. You are you. Article Seven, Redemption Tip Number Five."

"Don't go off book," snapped Heinrich.

"I am book," said Trubate.

"I am me," shouted Old Gold. He bounded down to Beach, cut his cuffs away, chased the air with elegant swipes of his knife. He had the bearing of some highborn reaper, a cruel dandy. He caught a piece of Beach's face and Beach snatched his wrist, judo'd his arm around, bent it to some inhuman parameter that got Old Gold howling. Beach took the knife now, put the blade to Old Gold's neck. Was he awaiting thumbs from Caesar's skybox? What a soldier, sailor. A shot boomed down from the porch, spun Beach, put him on his knees. He pawed at the hole in his shoulder, the wet epaulette of blood blooming there.

Old Gold laid his boot on Beach's back.

"Look at my fucking demon now!" he said. "Little Sissy demon! I am a cloudwalker and I rain my rain of piss down on your meek inheritor ass!"

Old Gold took his cock out, pinched it down towards Beach's skull. We waited for a while.

"No flow," said Old Gold.

We heard another shot and tiny flecks of Old Gold's ass went twirling into the lights.

"For real?" he said, and fainted. Heinrich tucked his pistol in his dinner jacket, started down the steps.

"And the moral of the story," he said, "is never mock your demon. A corollary to that moral would be never postpone square dance night. Now let's put this fiasco behind us. Tend to the wounded. Beach will be our brother, if he so chooses."

Most of us made to leave.

"You," said Heinrich. "Come walk with me."

We walked out toward some power lines. Past the lit perimeter was a night of huge near stars. They were greening themselves up there like those stick-on galaxies my mother used to buy for my bedroom ceiling, those stars that came with charts I was too lazy to learn.

"That's okay," she'd said, "just use your imagination. Make your own constellations. Gods and animals. Heroes and bears."

I had no idea what she could mean. I scattered the decals around in a way I thought looked natural, random, skylike.

"Just want to stretch my legs a little," Heinrich said now.

We walked out past the last of the cabins to the treeline. A breeze blew over the field. I wanted to hear ghost voices on it, bog plaints, heath pleas. Please Note, Please Note. A serious fucking prizewinner, that. But Wendell was still dead. And I was still dying, wasn't I? Who would note? What had *I* ever noted? I'd taken my pleasures, of course, I'd eaten the foods of the world, drunk my wine, put this or that forbidden particulate in my nose until the room lit up like a festival town and all my friends, but just my friends, were seers. I'd seen the great cities, the great lakes, the oceans and the so-called seas, slept in soft beds and awakened to fresh juice and fluffy towels and terrific water pressure. I'd fucked in moonlight, sped through desolate interstate kingdoms of high broken beauty, met wise men, wise women, even a wise movie star. I'd lain on lawns that, cut, bore the scent of rare spice. I'd ridden dune buggies, foreign rails. I'd tasted forty-five kinds of coffee, not counting decaf.

I hadn't put things off, I'd done them, just done them blind. Steady rain of ruin. Steady dark. You see too much and you can't see anything at all. You lose your beautiful wife to your cousin, or the sun. You beget hooligans. Or maybe you're the old man in the hospital, giving thanks to the Elks, the Black Kids, pressing the button, pressing it, but the girl never comes.

All my pretty ones.

Fuckeroo'd.

"Have you changed your mind about leaving?" said Heinrich.

"No," I said.

"No, he says," said Heinrich.

I heard noises behind us. Someone was squeezing me to the dirt. Someone was stuffing my head into a sleeve.

"Wait," I heard Heinrich say.

Wires poked my neck, my ears.

"What are you doing?"

"Notty, look how funny he looks with the beard."

Naperton stood near me while I stripped.

"Wish we had a boilersuit," he said. "We used to have a boilersuit. I don't know where the hell it's got to now. Can you see through the hood? Be honest."

"No," I said.

Something cracked at the back of my knee.

"Can't fault your honesty."

I curled up to the thatch.

"Have you ever seen those pictures of Chet Guevara all shot up to shit?"

"Che," I said.

"What?"

"Che Guevara."

"I'm not talking about him."

"Is this part of the mothering process?"

"This would be idle chatter," said Naperton. "Get up."

He bent my arms around a pole, cinched my wrists. I heard the thatch swish, a new pair of boots in the room.

"I'll take it from here, Notty," said Heinrich. "Better get on the road, beat traffic."

"Right."

I hung there sucking hood, listened to Heinrich putter around the hut. He moved quietly, methodically, like some neighbor in the next apartment on a Sunday afternoon. Tin pots, the dull hammering of picture hooks. I heard Heinrich stab at the fire, spread something out in the dirt, a tarp, perhaps, lob what sounded like a sack of metal on it.

"They sure were big on gadgets back in the bubonic days," said Heinrich. "The Breast Ripper. Purpose self-evident, I guess. Or the Branks. A sort of pierced tongue brace for the nagging missus. The Pear. Goes up your ass like a piece of fruit, splits open in your prostate. What I wish we had is a Judas Cradle, but those are a bitch to rig."

"What are you going to do to me?" I said.

"Judas Cradle. Sounds like one of those rock bands."

"Don't," I said. "Please."

"Don't what?"

"Please," I said.

The hut was a furnace now.

"Falanga," Heinrich said. "I love that word. Falanga. The beating of the soles of the feet. Submarino is water torture, near drowning. Very big in Uruguay when I was down there. Fellow up at Harvard or someplace, he did a study, took regular people, housewives, students, told them to shock someone in the next room. He'd have actors in there pretending to be in agony. Most of them kept turning up the volts. Even with the screams, the pleas. What do you think of that?"

"Doctor's orders."

"That's right," said Heinrich. "But now it's all about deprivation. That's the thing nowadays. No light, no air, no sleep, no
food, no water. Or just food. Dry food. Stale peanuts. Stale
saltines. No water. Cotton mouth. Or kick a blindfolded man
off a chopper. How could he possibly know he's only a few feet
off the ground? The complex of emotions when he hits, that's
what breaks him. These are the techniques. The state of the
art. Make somebody stand for days. Fluids collect in the feet.
Believe me, you can't conceive of the pain. You can't conceive
of the fluids. It's not about violating the body anymore. It's
about putting the subject in a situation whereby the subject's
body violates him. Betrays him. Do you get this distinction?
It's kind of subtle."

"It's not so subtle."

"You're a subtle man. How did you like tomorrow? I used
to see that on billboards when we made cheese runs. Somebody
wrote that crap, I always said."

"Me."

"Yes, you."

"So, that's the deal?"

"What's that?"

"Deprivation?"

"No," said Heinrich. "You've already been so deprived."

What he did to me now he did for a good long time. He did
it maybe with some of the tools he'd talked about, the ones
from the tarp, the grand antiques, the hooks and prongs and
pincers I heard him pull from the fire. Sometimes he did it
with his hands. The lulls were the worst part. Too much time
to smell the cook stench.

I blacked out, came up into some throb of wakefulness. My

hood was slipping and I saw pieces of the room. Heinrich knelt in the corner with an old Army-issue hand crank telephone. He clipped leads to it, ran the wires back to where I hung.

"Steve," he said, "I'm really thinking you've earned a phone privilege."

He went back to the corner and turned the crank.

I woke up next to the dead fire, my cuffs cut away. There was a note in one of my shoes: "Welcome to the World of Self-Born Men. P.S. Given your condition, you are relieved of kitchen duty for the rest of the week."

I stumbled out of the hut, fell a few times running down the hill trail, ripped my shins on roots and stones. My bones were making soft, sifting noises. I had to blow blood from my nose to breathe.

Old Gold stood at the gate. He'd gotten his knife out, and by his expression appeared to be already picturing some triumphal display of my pancreas.

"Come to keep me company?" he said.

"I'm walking through this gate, Gold."

"My job will be to stop you."

"Fair enough," I said. "But there's something you should keep in mind. I have nothing to lose. I'm a fucking terminal. Doesn't that resonate with you?"

"Folks who really got nothing to lose, they just go ahead and do the stuff they want to do, Steve. They sure as shit don't make speeches about it."

"All right," I said. "What if I forget about the gate? What if I go through the trees?"

"Trees is fine," said Old Gold. "My thing is here at the gate."

"Bless you for your thing," I said.

I cut back around the dining hall, hacked through some poison sumac to the road. Now I'd have rashes in my wounds. Well, sure, why not? What kind of hellishness stinted on rashes? I stood out past the gate, looked back towards the compound, the blunted cone of Mount Redemption rising up behind it. I'd never found out if it was the cure or the disease that would cure me of my disease. Fat chance I ever would. I watched Old Gold punch the gate post for a while. Ninety-seven. Ninety-eight.

He saw me, waved.

Items #5

Pangburn Falls was a ghost of itself, a dead old barge town. I walked the main drag, boulevard of broken riverine hope, decrepit colonials, clapboard rot. Ancient porches slid down to junkyard lawns. Bent bicycles, rusted barbells, bladeless fans. All my father's owner's manual agon ended in this place. Here rested the gadget dead. I heard a whinny, a snort. Down the street a palomino drank from an inflatable kiddie pool.

There was a gas station up ahead, warm window neon, a lit sign spinning in the mist. They were advertising something called half-serve at the pumps. Some men stood near a tow rig with hot coffee and crullers.

"Hey, look," said one in coveralls. "It's a bust-out."

I readied for flight. I wondered if I had it in me for sustained fleeing. There was a shopping mall on the other side of the river. Parking lot, pink stucco, brick. What would I do if I got there? Hide behind a rack of sport coats? Beg the grill cooks for a fry boy hat?

One of the men by the tow rig made a hard fart.

"Dragon tail," he said, darted into the repair bay.

"How's the freak life, freak?" said a kid with long hair and T-shirt that read: *I Skull-Fucked Your Dead Mother Today, What'd You Do?*

Must share a mail-order club with Parish, I thought.

"I'm tired of the freak life, tell you the truth," I said.

I tried to coo it country.

"Where you from?" said the man in coveralls.

"South of here."

"South you mean the city?"

"Yeah."

"I got a daughter there."

"Doubt I know her."

"What, you think I'm some kind of moron?"

"No."

"I'm just letting you know that I sympathize."

"Sympathize?"

"Fish out of water," he said.

"Fish a-floppin'," said the kid with the T-shirt. "Ready for the blade de filet."

"Blade de what?" said the first man. "Don't mind Donald. He's stifled. My name's Steve."

"They call me that, too," I said.

Steve led me back through the repair bay.

"Take a load off. I'll get some coffee. Cream?"

"Thanks."

I fell asleep in the chair. Later someone was shaking me awake. Steve handed me a mug of coffee, leaned back on a gunmetal desk littered with invoice slips. I checked the cup for advertising slogans. Ancient reflex, I guess. *Steve's Auto Repair*, it said, *Fixin' Since Nixon.*

Rookies.

"We got one of you guys a few years ago," said Steve. "Looked like hell. Told us some crazy shit about how he'd failed to be a good mother, something like that. What's that about? It sounded somehow faggot-related. Like from the urban gay subculture."

"I'm not sure what it's about," I said.

"I'm not a homophobic, you know."

"I didn't know that," I said.

"Got a brother in the bi-lifestyle."

"Look," I said. "I'm not sure what it's all about. All I know is I've got to get back to the city."

"Reminds me of before. When old Heinrich had the prison camp. Better than a real prison, far as business around here went. Too bad he got all artsy fartsy. Though it looks like he's still getting his licks in. Boy, are you a sight. You know, my pops was on the march to Bataan."

"Can I use your phone?" I said.

"You know about Bataan?"

"I saw a movie."

"The movie captured about one percent of the horror, my friend."

"I got the idea, though."

"And about three percent of the idea."

"I'm sorry about Bataan. Tell your father I'm sorry about it."

"I will. That's kind of you. Guess I'll go over to the cemetery this afternoon and inform him of your concern. Want to come, asshole? Phone's right there."

I called Fiona.

"Daddy, where are you?"

"I'm in hell, baby," I said.

"Is there a bus?" said Fiona.

"Is there a bus?" I asked Steve.

"Of course there's a bus," he said.

Fiona put fifty-three dollars' worth of motor oil she would never need on her mother's credit card. Steve counted out the cash.

"If you'd been more knowledgeable about Jap atrocities," he said, "I just might have given you the dough for the ticket straight up. But you see my predicament."

The bus didn't leave for a few hours. I hitched a ride with Donald to the hospital.

"I'm going that way, anyway," he said. "You might want to get some stitches or something. Or a body cast."

"I like your T-shirt," I said.

"It's meant to be provocative," he said. "I'm not really such a bad guy. I'm just stifled."

Local needlepoint adorned the walls of the Pangburn Falls Medical Clinic like cheery exhortations to liver failure. Everything stank of Lysol and meaningless neighborly death. An enormous woman in stretch pants approached me with a wooden clipboard and a pencil with a fluffy feather on it.

"Name, insurance company, complaint," she said.

Then she looked up from her clipboard.

"Oh my fucking word," she said.

The needlepoint sampler on the far wall read "God's on Duty." I studied it for days, maybe more than days, that pale stitchwork, those fleeces of cloudbank at the corners. When I felt up to moving my eyes a bit I commenced analysis of the fiberboard panels in the ceiling—like snowflakes, no two chemical flecks were alike—and the tulips going to dead rot on the windowsill.

My head was halo'd, stilled with welds. The rest of me was set in traction, some kind of high-tech mold.

A woman walked into my room, laid her hand on my mold.

"A man's home is his cast," she said.

I said nothing.

"Don't say anything," said the woman. "My name is Dr. Cornwallis. You've been severely injured. You're lucky the shock got you here. Now did you understand that the first thing I said to you was a pun? Do you like puns?"

My eyes went tulipward.

"Don't shake your head," said Dr. Cornwallis. "Nobody really likes puns. Even the good ones grate. There's a theory that chronic punning is a neurological disorder. Blink if you find that hypothesis remotely intriguing. Blink if you wish me to speak in less mannered style."

I was mute for another month.

. . .

Then I said something, a word.

The night nurse said the word was Steve. She said this the next night. Steve was her dead son's name, and she wanted to know if he'd given me any kind of message to deliver before Jesus released me on my own recognizance, as he sometimes did, when someone dies but still has a job to do, like deliver a message.

"Steve said to say he loves you," I said.

"That's it?"

"He's sorry he didn't listen to you more. About drugs and stuff. You know, how you shouldn't do them until you fall in love."

I felt suddenly groggy.

"I feel suddenly groggy," I said.

"How did he look?" said the night nurse.

"Who?" I said.

"My boy."

"The light was too bright. All I saw was this bright light."

I noticed now I was out of the mold, could use my hands. I used them to shape the idea of light.

"How did he sound?" said the night nurse.

"Like heavenly-like."

"What else?"

"Wings," I said.

"Wings?"

"Wings," I said.

The night nurse wiped my halo with a fold of gauze.

"Golly," she said. "Your holes look infected."

She pushed the gauze through a flap in the wall.

"What do you mean?" I said.

She stood, rolled my tray away.

"What if I need to reach my tray?" I said.

"What if?" said the night nurse. She used her hands to make the shape of if, or maybe it was what.

I waited for the day nurse.

Dr. Cornwallis poked her head into my room.

"I'm just poking my head in," she said.

"Okay," I said.

"How are you feeling?"

"Not so hot," I said.

"I wouldn't think so," said Dr. Cornwallis. "I'd be hard pressed to believe you if you told me you were feeling hot. That's what I told Sally. I told Sally you've been traumatized, and as a result you've experienced severe trauma. I'm talking about the wings incident. May I extend an apology on your behalf?"

"Extend," I said.

"Excellent," said Dr. Cornwallis. "Is there anything else I can do for you?"

"My tray."

"I'll get someone to come push it closer," said Dr. Cornwallis.

"Can't you do it?"

"I wish I could."

"Maybe God could do it," I said. "He's on duty."

"That's a joke, right?" said Dr. Cornwallis.

"Yes," I said.

"No, I just wanted to make sure it wasn't a pun."

. . .

The day nurse was Donald, the stifled guy from the gas station. He walked in, winked, rolled my tray back to my bed. He had his hair up in pigtails, a pentagram pinned to his scrubs.

"Don't worry about the dead kid thing," said Donald. "Sally's all hung up on her dead kid."

"How'd he die?" I said.

"Kid-type thing. Chased a ball into the street. Me, I have children, they aren't getting any balls, that's for sure. No balls, no horseshoes, none of that shit."

"Do you remember me?" I said.

"Sure. From the Shell. You looked even worse then."

"How do I look now?"

"Like you chased a ball into the street."

"Can I see? Can you bring me a mirror?"

"I'd advise against it," said Donald. "Maybe down the road."

I pointed up at the pentagram.

"Satan?" I said.

"Donald," said Donald.

Dr. Cornwallis poked her head into my room.

"Just thought I'd poke my head in," she said.

"Poke away," I said.

"We need to talk."

"Let's talk," I said.

"It's about your finances, or lack thereof. Your coverage has expired."

"I've reached the maximum amount of maximum expenditure."

"That's what I've been given to understand by Ms. Kincaid."

"My old pen pal."

"You're going to have to leave, I'm afraid."

"You can't do that," I said.

"We do it all the time."

"What about your hypocritical oath?"

"Now that's a pun."

"Sorry," I said.

"I've fulfilled my oath. I've treated you for your injuries. I can't help it if you have a preexisting condition."

"Preexisting?" I said.

The doctor pulled a shiny book from her doctor pocket.

PREXIS: THE RACE AGAINST PERSONAL EXTINCTION
by Leon Goldfarb, M.D., and Vaughn Blackstone, D.D.S.

"Blackstone's a dentist?" I said.

"I know the cover looks a little gaudy," said Dr. Cornwallis, "but it's quite a good book. It was given to me by a man who works at the alternative healing outreach program here at the hospital. We're trying to widen the scope of our treatment. Maybe there's a place for you there. Wen said there might be a place for you there."

"Wen?"

"Wendell Tarr is his name."

"The Wanderer Wendell," I said.

"Oh, he pretty much stays around here. Anyway, the alternative program is really your only alternative, given your lack of coverage. We make exceptions in the alternative program with regard to coverage, whereas in the traditional—"

"Okay," I said.

"Wonderful," said Dr. Cornwallis. "Now get out of bed. Let's see if you can walk."

I could walk. Waddle, rather. I could bend a bit, swivel, squat. It hurt. Not like it hurt in the hut, but it hurt. I figured I'd shake out the pain for a minute, make a dash for it, the door.

I made a dash for the door. Dr. Cornwallis had to call Donald in from the hall. He picked me up, toweled me off where I'd pissed my gown.

"Thanks," I said.

"It's what I do," said Donald.

The next morning I had a visitor. He stood near the window for a while, sniffed the dead flowers, glanced up, glided over. There was something of the sea in him. A man who swam with dolphins, maybe, manatees. I could see us underwater near a reef. We weren't talking. We were squeaking. We were genius mammals of the sea. Then the gentleman started talking.

"Call me Wen," he said.

"The Wanderer Wendell," I said.

"Call me Wen," said the Wanderer.

"Wen," I said.

"You need to get well," he said. "In all ways. I'd like to escort you now to the Alternative Outreach Wing. But it's really inreach, really. I want to say that up front. Any questions?"

"Yes," I said. "Aren't you supposed to be dead?"

"Aren't you?"

"No, I mean they talk about you. Please note."

"You liked that," said Wen.

"Yeah."

"Mythology. Schoolyard stuff. Remember the kid who stuck his hand out the bus window?"

"Got lopped off."

"Did it?" said Wen.

He held up his hand at a squid-like tilt.

"It's right here," he said. "The motion it's making means come with me."

I followed him down some dingy corridors. We passed more needlepoint, doors ajar to sun-soaked rooms.

"Right up here," said Wen. He slapped his palm on a button on the wall. The button was palm-sized. A pair of glass doors parted.

"By the way, we don't use painkillers in this wing."

"What do you use?"

"For what?"

Wen took me to a room like my room in the other wing, but no needlepoint.

He said to get some rest. We'd begin that afternoon.

"Begin what?"

"That's your decision," said Wen.

"What do you suggest?"

"Well, you're dying. Maybe we should deal with that first."

"I'm not dying," I said.

"Au contraire, amigo," said Wen.

He flipped the PREXIS book onto my bed. The chrome type on his copy had a slightly different tint, a blurb emblazoned across the top—" 'Read it before your line dies out!'—Dr. Lauren Lovinger."

"Peruse at your leisure," said Wen.

I got into bed and started to leaf through the preface.

Not surprisingly, it was only after the results of the most routine of checkups for the most routine of men were faxed to us with some peculiar queries, that the hunt for PREXIS really began. . . . The subject had an admittedly rough time adjusting to the truth of his condition . . . countless blind alleys and false starts later the race was on! . . . Maybe I wasn't a circus caliber juggler, but I was good enough to dream. . . . Like the proverbial horse of proverb, you can lead a man to the laboratory, but you can't make him fully confront the implications of the data. . . . Nobody, of course, with our current technological capabilities, can really know what death feels like. . . .

I drifted off hearing Heinrich's voice.

"Falanga," it said. "Oh, dear Christ, sing it, Falanga!"

Lem Burke was at the window when I woke. He was squeezing whiteheads through his chin fuzz, putting the pus up to sunlight, making odd snorts I took for empirical glee.

"Breakthrough?" I said.

Lem flicked his pore goo at the window pane.

"Morning."

"Never thought I'd see you again," I said.

"How much did you think about it?"

"Are you here with your mother?"

"Figured she'd give Wendell a whirl," he said. "She's a guru addict, I guess."

"We all need love," I said.

"Bullshit," said Lem. "We all need bullshit."

I did have pity for the kid. Born in a bubble of babble, shuttled from one freak retreat to the next. So knowing, but what did he know? Estelle once claimed to have home-schooled him. I think that meant she gave him a couple of coloring books, left him alone to talk to himself.

"I'm supposed to take you to group."

Lem led me down to an airy dayroom. People in pajamas sat in slat-backed chairs. Wen was there, wearing a sweater with tiny felt animals sewn on it.

"My name is Wen," he said, "and I'm feeling what I'm feeling today."

I took a seat, looked around at all this pain, puff-eyed, in flame-retardant cotton.

There's an air hockey table in the dayroom, and when I'm not too busy feeling what I'm feeling, I'm taking Lem in three-out-of-fives for the day-old doughnuts Nurse Donald sneaks us from the cafeteria. Cudahy and I used to play on a table just like this one in his father's basement, until the Thornfield boys took a clawhammer to it. The world is full of sore losers. Some go on to win with great bitterness, too. Me, I've just always loved the sound of these babies warming up, all that air hockey air jetting up through holes.

Lem's nom de puck is The Wrist. I'm Rip Van Winkie, maybe on account of the new white shoots in my hair. Today there was a coconut flake on the line, but the game was called due to an unscheduled shame rap. Out came the chairs of sharing. The pajama zombies filed in.

"I'm feeling less than today," Wen said, picked at the fuzzy rhino on his sleeve. "My shame monster has woken from deep slumber."

A hard, thin pain slung through me as he spoke.

"Steve," said Wen. "Are you okay? You're shaking over there."

"I'm fine, Wen," I said.

"We all know what that means," said the woman beside me. Estelle Burke. Scorned ballerina. She tore at her thumb with her teeth.

"It doesn't mean anything," I said. "Do we have to do this now?"

"Wen's shame monster reared up," said Estelle. "You can't just pick and choose when that's going to happen."

"Thank you, Estelle," said Wen.

"Yes, thank you," I said, "for the blowjob Wen is about to receive."

"Whoa!" said Estelle. "I mean, from where?"

She spit some cuticle on my knee.

"It's okay," said Wen.

"Fuck okay," said Estelle. "I'm feeling very flanked."

"I understand the flanked feeling," said Wen. "And I understand Steve's rage. Though I can't condone it."

"I don't feel so good," I said.

"In what sense?" said Wen.

I had a fairly heady answer planned before I pitched off the chair.

"Steve?" said Wen.

"My name's not Steve," I said from the floor.

"What is it then?" said Lem.

"John Q. Fuckeroo."

"Is that Welsh?" said Estelle. "My first husband was Welsh."

"I'm the stewman," I said.

Everyone stared.

Wen walked me back to my door.

"You've got to stop collapsing," he said. "It's impeding your progress."

I found Lem down near the bed sifting through some dust balls.

"What's going on?" I said.

"Nothing," said Lem. "I dropped some Percodan."

"Where'd you get Percodan?"

"Your nurse buddy, Donald. Decent caring Donald."

"I'm going home, Lem," I said. "I'm going home to live or die but I'm going home."

"Probably die," said Lem.

"You're coming with me."

"I can't," said Lem. "I'm a country boy."

"You're a freak, Lem. A botched psychosocial experiment."

"I'm not that bad. I get the jokes on TV."

"We have to stick together now."

"I have to find the percs I dropped."

"You didn't drop them. No one ever drops anything."

"What's these, then?" said Lem.

We popped the pills, broke out some Bavarian creams. We rolled the TV in from the TV lounge.

"I've seen this," I said.

"Don't ruin it," said Lem.

Sandhogs ate their sandwiches and died by the score. The host stood inside the tiled tube, sobbed.

"The men were mealed," he said. "Until a granular quality obtained."

Items #6

We took a bus down to the city with the motor oil money. We got a good movie on the bus. It was about airplanes falling out of the sky. Airplanes fell, boats sank, what could you do but get nervous? Buses swerved into ditches, mostly, or they tumbled from mountaintops in mountainous countries and only the chickens lived. But the chickens, they'd get buried in an avalanche. The avalanche would kick off a flood. Rivers would swell, whole villages would be wiped out. It was horrible, horrible. These goddamn countries were exporting horror and they had to be stopped. Maybe invaded, even.

I mentioned my concern to Lem.

"You're out of your fucking mind," he said. "It's the PREXIS. It's snacking on your faculty for reason."

"I'm in fine fettle," I said.

But I'd been feeling the shoots and shudders again. The organ-flutter, the vein ache. Lem had his perc stash in his fanny pack. I partook, feared more chicken visions.

We pulled into Port Authority at dusk. The home grime gladdened me. I led Lem through the throng.

"How about a peep show?"

"It's all kiddie stuff now," I said.

"Kiddie porn?"

"Kind of."

I shoved him onto a downtown train.

"Gibbering, jostling humanity," said Lem.

"Sit the fuck down," I said.

A man stood near us gripping the pole. He dropped his pants, groaned down into a squat.

"I have no place to shit tonight," he said. "Can you help me find a place to shit tonight?"

He started to pass a hat around.

"Have you ever really done it?" Lem asked the man.

"Done what?"

"Taken a dump on the train."

"That's disgusting," said the man.

It looked like they were doing some work on my old building. There were ladders outside, high bins full of stones. The neighborhood had been crumbling for some time. Every so often a gargoyle would topple off an edifice, crush a schoolgirl. It was good homegrown horror but people still preferred the imported kind. My old neighbor, an architect, wore a hard hat everywhere outside. He called us all cornice-bait.

Lem and I walked into the lobby and waited for the elevator.

"You're not going to believe this," said Lem, "but I've never been on one of these before."

"An elevator?"

"People fuck in them, right?"

"Constantly."

We got in with an old lady I used to bathe.

"Hilda," I said.

"Hilda's dead," said the woman. "I'm Hilda's mother."

My apartment door had been painted over. Someone was doing slap bass scales inside. I knocked and a woman in platinum-rimmed safety glasses answered the door. She had a jar of ointment with her. The label said Rad Balm. She daubed some of it on her lips.

"What?" she said.

"I live here," I said.

"Are you a time traveler?"

"I don't understand."

"Maybe you used to live here."

"That's very clever," I said. "How'd you get in?"

"Super gave me the key."

The Rad Balm girl disappeared, came back with a cardboard box. There was my Jews of Jazz calendar sticking out, Cudahy's track jacket, some spice vials bound in rubber band.

"Yours?"

"Yes."

"I had no real reason to save it. No law compelled me. And how many months does Benny Goodman get anyway?"

"Somebody gave me that calendar."

"Somebody gave me chlamydia. Stop making excuses. You'll be better off."

"I'd be better off if I hadn't been illegally evicted from my home."

"That I can't help you with. Just the emotional stuff."

"Thanks," I said. "See you around."

"Sure."

"You play beautifully," said Lem.

"It's not me," said the Rad Balm girl. "It's software for the fish."

"Fish?" said Lem.

"That's musician talk."

She shut the door.

We got some hot dogs and papaya juice, sat with the pigeons in a park. The park was mostly concrete. Stone benches, stone fountains, a brick chute for the kids. I threw a piece of wiener to the birds. They didn't mob it the way I'd hoped. A few made some listless pecks. It was a slowdown.

"Get hungry later," said Lem, "we can always eat one of those guys."

"Full of disease."

"Glass houses, pal."

Traffic was jammed up at the intersection. Stop-and-go all the way to the bridge. Families on the other side of the river were probably boiling their dinner pouches, cursing the tardi-

ness of their pouch-winners. Surly sons punched down the
channel changer for some late-afternoon bikini tit before Mom
came home. Disaffected daughters carved Wiccan proverbs
into their arms. Cats dozed on quilts, recovering traumatic
memories in dream. Most cats were once mishandled kittens.
This was all waiting for the men and women in the cars and
they leaned on their horns as though they did not know they
were already home.

I decided to die. I figured I owed it to myself, maybe to future personal extinction victims everywhere. Cleaved, sawed,
prised open, my corpse would yield the secret to their salvation.
Maybe it was fair penance for the damage I'd done.

Tough cookies.

"Come on," I said to Lem. "I've got to make a call."

We took a train back up to Port Authority. We had an
hour to kill before the next bus, found a lone porn shop tucked
off near a parking lot. New laws had reconfigured the stock.
Teen comedy up near the register, teen anal in back. Somehow
it reminded me of a medieval synagogue I'd once visited in
Spain.

Tenakill was a leafy ville out past the city limits. The plaque at
the bus stand explained the name was Dutch but that the
Dutch had left before explaining what it meant.

Maryse was out by the curb in what must have been the
latest in suburban transport. You could see where the gun
mounts had gone, how you might secure the wounded. The
color was a cousin to teal. We climbed in back and Maryse
nodded, peeled out toward the hills. The vehicle shook with
Bach.

"You used to call this math rock," I said.

"I appreciate it now," she said. "I'm a much more evolved appreciator."

We passed a chain video store and a shop selling "locally scented" candles. The Latte Da, Tenakill's most stylish café, advertised an open mike sonnet slam to benefit victims of the victim culture.

"By the way," I said, "this is Lem."

"Okay, Lem," said Maryse.

"Thanks for picking us up," I said.

"I take it this isn't just a friendly visit."

"I think we're being very friendly," I said.

"Look," said Lem, pointed out the window. "It's a white person."

"Kid's a comedy gem," said Maryse.

Business news burbled out of the wall. William was asleep on modular suede. His laptop was sliding off his lap. His slipper had fallen to the carpet. There were bruises on his toes.

"Oh," said William, waking. "Hey. Hi. Wow. Look at you. Hey. Hi. Come sit down."

"He called before," said Maryse. "I didn't want to interrupt you."

"Trading in my sleep," said William. "Nap trader."

"He hasn't told me why he's here," said Maryse. "He said he wanted to speak to the both of us. Coffee?"

"Coffee," said William. "Terrific. Coffee?"

"I'm in," said Lem.

"He's in. Terrific."

William looked down at his swollen toes.

"Thought we had a creep," he said. "A prowler. I kicked the credenza."

We sat quietly for a while. William seemed to be conducting vital transactions on his laptop. I peered over, watched him switch his desktop photo from a seascape to an apple basket. Lem was scoping the stock quotes on the wall screen. He had this look on his face, some annihilating wonderment.

"Has anyone ever explained this stuff to you?" I said.

"What, why the biotechs are diving?"

Maryse came back with a tray full of cappuccinos.

"Cinnamon?" she said. "Nutmeg? I recommend cardamom."

"She's never wrong about this shit," said William. "Am I right?"

"We used to drink instant," I said.

"Is that true, honey?"

"God," said Maryse. "I can hardly remember. Could be. It's the kind of life we were leading."

"So," said William, "what brings you to Tenakill? Not that we're not thrilled to see you. Especially, you know, considering. I mean you're really bearing up, aren't you? I mean, under the weight. The weight of your illness. Is illness okay?"

"I'm not," I said.

"Not what?"

"I'm not really bearing up. I'm gearing down. Do you get what I mean? That lap you run after the race is over?"

"The victory lap?"

"Not that one," I said.

"The cool-down," said Maryse.

"That's it," I said. "The cool-down. My race is run. Do you understand what I'm saying?"

"Wow," said William. "Terrific. I mean, not terrific. I mean the opposite of terrific. Do you need money? I have money."

"I know you have money."

"It's well known, I guess," said William. "My frugality is less documented. But I can do something for you. Some cash. A check. We'll call it a loan but only to call it something. Look, you're my friend. A friend is forever. Or until there's a problem with the friendship. But this isn't about friendship anyway. I can see that. Where are my glasses?"

"I don't think he wants money," said Maryse. "Am I right?"

"Yes," I said.

"I think he wants more than money. Am I correct?"

"Yes," I said.

"More than money is tough for me right now," said William.

I took a sip of cappuccino, coughed it up into the cup.

"That's not cardamom," said Maryse.

"Looks like blood," said Lem.

They gave me the guest room.

The guilt room, I heard William call it from the hallway. He'd have to work on his whisper.

His portfolio was in good shape, he told me, even in the wake of Cruel April, that rash of crashes last spring, and I was not to fret expenses. Besides, he'd had a little chat with Leon Goldfarb. Arrangements to ease various individual and collective burdens were in the offing.

"What does that mean?"

"You tell me," said William. "It sounded like Jew talk."

"Watch it," I said.

"Don't be a child," said William. "My uncle hid yids in Rotterdam."

"You never told me that."

"You never asked."

"What part of the war was this?"

"What war? This was the early seventies."

The guilt room was a good room.

I got fresh flowers, fresh linen, fresh fruit, audiotapes of tides and typhoons, waterfalls, gales, natural sounds to confirm one's droplet status in the eternal downpour. I got satellite TV, a universal remote, a Dictaphone for last words if the ligature of my pen hand failed.

I got my daughter, bedside, reading me box scores and poems. I couldn't fathom the math of either, but Fiona's voice eased the pain somehow. Maybe the pills did, too.

I sensed something torrid going on between Lem and my little girl. The idea made me glad. I liked to picture them in faraway rooms, confessing their secrets, flaunting their moles, vaulting themselves into some soulful teen future. William's place was enormous so I never saw those rooms. I was bedbound, mostly, or wheelchair'd when my color was up and I could join them all for a few minutes at table, feign delight in food.

I was dying well, could detect a certain shimmer in the mirror, a made-for-TV terminal glow. I was going to light up the land with love and forgiveness, die with a wide wise grin. Angels in work casual sweaters would chaperon my ascent to paradise. Maybe my soul would return on occasion, spook my family into betterment. I'd smash a vase or burn a curtain and Fiona would finally know that nicotine was addictive, that sex with her soccer coach had repercussions.

Maryse was spooning broth through my teeth when she said she thought Fiona was no longer disaffected.

"She's flourishing," said Maryse.

"She's grown," I said.

"Lem seems like a good boy."

"He has a good heart."

"He's a little odd, though," said Maryse. "Is he on drugs?"

"Usually," I said.

"I guess people can change."

"Have I?"

"Have you what?"

"Changed."

"I see an arc," said Maryse. "A trajectory."

"Really?"

"Maybe not," said Maryse. "But sometimes it's about how you transform the people around you. Sometimes someone has to be the messenger."

"Is that me?"

"No," said Maryse.

"Who am I, then?"

"You're Steve."

"I refuse that," I said. "Even as life refuses me."

"Maybe it's not a refusal, Steve," said Maryse. "Maybe there is a higher power and he or she or it has plans for you."

"Do you believe that?"

"No," said Maryse.

"Van Winkie," said Lem, from the doorway.

"The Wrist," I said.

Lem sat down, chucked me under the chin.

"I just want to say that whatever happens, I'll take care of Fiona. I don't want you to worry about her."

"We know what's going to happen."

"Either way," said Lem.

"Okay," I said. "Either way."

"Do you want some morphine?"

"I'm fine."

"Do you mind if I have some?" said Lem. "You know, the stress. My girlfriend's dad is dying."

"Okay," I said. "Do me, too."

The Philosopher and the Mechanic dropped by for occasional visits. Transition maintenance, I heard the Mechanic call it.

Departure management, the Philosopher said.

It'd been nearly two years since my checkup.

"Do you remember when we first diagnosed you?" said the Philosopher.

"Sure."

"The salad days."

It was a time for testimonials, recollections, goodbyes, Godspeeds.

William the Fulfiller wanted absolution.

"What happened with me and Maryse, I know how much pain we caused you. It's tragic the way happiness hurts others."

"It's okay."

"We're happy," he said.

"I know."

"But it hurt you."

"Yes, it did."

"Exactly," he said. "I just wanted to be sure."

The Philosopher and the Mechanic said it could be any day. There was no way to calculate. By their calculations there could be no calculations. Me, I was on the uptick, the pain on slow fade, a new feeling in my veins, a deep living slither. People would be disappointed. I began to flutter my eyelids a bit, affect a weak grip, mutter cryptic phrases tinged with tiny history, a Dutch Schultz delirium of baby talk and birch nest slaughter.

"Cudahy," I said, "don't burn them, they're butterflies!"

"Who's the navigator? I'm the navigator. I'm the snack-giver. I'm your mommy in snacks."

"Some companies make powerful computers. We make powerful people."

"Perhaps the most prevalent trope in fire safety literature is the notion of the regrouping area. The family gathers at a point distant enough from the conflagration to prevent a singeing or charring of the ideation of domesticity."

"Vast gulfs may be received on vast gulf days. One radio equals one radio nation. I heard the tittering of Velcro. Naperton's grapefruit brain, my pupilage. True puny. Renee, Renee, my rivulet . . ."

"Can't be long now," said the Mechanic.

"Is this all some kind of gag?"

Fiona sang to me, softly, our aardvark song:

> *Aardvark*
> *Lovely aardvark*
> *I have only the vaguest sense*
> *Of what you look like*
> *I know there's a nose*
> *That works like a hose*
> *Beyond that*
> *I just have certain cultural associations*

It was really more of a spoken-word piece.

"Daddy?" said Fiona.

"Yes, darling?"

"Do you remember when I was really sick and you ran through the streets with me in your arms?"

"My doll-daughter."

"What?"

"I remember."

"Do you think I suffered any brain damage from the fever?"

"What?"

"Sometimes I feel like I'm not as smart as I should be."

"You're almost a genius, Fiona."

"And I have to live with that *almost* every day of my life."

"I'm sorry, baby. But I think you're just fine."

"Daddy, when you're dead, I'm going to be so fucking pissed at you. Do you know that? It's a grief mechanism, or whatever, but I'm really going to hate your fucking guts for a while. It'll take a long time to work it all through. I've already warned Lem. He's okay with it. Lem is amazing, Daddy. Thank you for bringing him to me. He's like some kind of inner astronaut. He drifts along in the deep space of his consciousness like no one I've ever been with before. Daddy, do you know what I mean when I say 'been with'? I mean, of course you know. But that's the thing about euphemisms. Most of them are true. Ha! That's pretty funny. But what I really mean, Daddy, is have you ever pictured me being with someone? I know fathers and daughters are supposed to have this bond, I mean, I know they do, even when I was at my most disaffected and had to be boarded at the School for it, even then I felt it, Daddy, and I think we're all adult enough to allow that there's got to be some sexual element inherent in this bond, Daddy, but people tend to leave off right there, don't they? For good reason, I guess. But really, have you ever really pictured it? Like have you ever pictured me being pussy-licked, say? Or maybe titty-tugged? Butt-banged? Clit-bit? Have you, Daddy? Did any of those particular pictures ever light up your inner astronaut viewing screen? Me on my knobby knees, cooz up in the air like a hairy flower, some big cock, some huge anonymous fuck stick jabbing into my tight, wet, almost-genius-caliber twat, me moaning and bucking, moaning and bucking—"

I took her hand, tenderly.

"Ow."

"Not really," I said.

"I'm going to hate you when you're dead, Daddy. It's a fact. Are you going to be all right with that?"

"Fiona," I said.

"I hate you now. Why did you have to be such a bad father?"

"I wasn't so bad."

"You were less than bad, which is worse. I'm fifteen fucking years old. What am I going to do without my fucked-up Daddy?"

She reached for me under the bedsheet.

"You watch," she said, "when you're dead I'm going to cut it off and put it in my ballerina box."

"Fiona!" I said. "Stop!"

Lem burst into the room.

"What's going on?" he said.

"Lem," said Fiona, "have you seen my ballerina box?"

Now the PERPS were popping up. People With PREXIS, all over the news. A rash of them in Wichita, in Wilmington, in Bakersfield, Dubuque. But this was not the crisis predicted, the plague ordained. They weren't dying. They were suing. Class action of the Infortunate.

"We're going after the charlatans," a federal prosecutor announced on the evening news. "This disease is nothing but a marketing ploy. Show me one death from PREXIS! Just one! It's time to close this shop down and show the world who the real perps are!"

The Mechanic came to see me.

"We're counting on you," he said. "Don't fuck it up."

"If you tell me not to fuck it up," I said, "I'll fuck it up."

"Then hang in there, dammit."

"What if I'm not dying?" I said.

"We've been through this before," said the Mechanic. "You're absolutely dying. But the ball's in your court."

That night Maryse wheeled me out to the dining room. The good linen was on the table, the good silver, the good silver napkin rings. There were bottles of burgundy, roses in a cut-glass vase, a rare roast garnished with parsley. I dipped my thumb in the gravy boat, licked it, swooned. Even the twine that bound the meat was beautiful.

"What's the occasion?" I said.

William dickered with a video camera mounted on a tripod in the corner, panned from roast to roses to me.

"I saw this on a TV special about dying," said Maryse. "Everyone gathers for a nice meal. It's the classy way to say goodbye."

"I'm not hungry," I said.

"Do it for Fiona," said Maryse. "The footage might prove useful down the line."

"Did you make yams?" I said.

"No, that's Thanksgiving."

"I just thought, you know, in honor of the time you kissed Cudahy."

"Why can't you let things go?"

"Because I don't have to. Because it seems they just leave of their own accord."

"You drove me away," said Maryse.

"As I remember it, William drove you away in his fucking convertible."

"Can you say that again, Steve?" said William. "I want to try the zoom."

"I hate all of you," I said.

"Wow," said William. "I'm right in there. I know the zoom is hackneyed, but when you're actually controlling it, it's very compelling."

Maryse took my wrist.

"When you're dead you won't feel that way," she said.

Fiona walked in wearing something diaphanous, nearly vampiric, a paste pearl choker at her throat. She led Lem by the elbow to his chair.

"Look," she said, "it's like we're an unconventional but loving family again."

"What exactly is a tilt?" said William. "It's just basically you tilt it, right?"

"Daddy," she said, "I'm sorry about before. It was the strain."

"It's okay, baby," I said.

"I'm ready to let go now, though."

"Baby," I said, "maybe I'm not ready."

"Sorry to interrupt, but . . ."

"But what?" I said.

William lifted his wineglass.

"I want to begin this dinner," he said, "by offering a few words on behalf of our guest of honor. It may be that I've known him longer than anyone here, and in so many ways he's the man I have to thank for my happiness. I can only hope that my friendship has brought him some measure of solace and/or bliss over the years as well. We've been through a lot together, haven't we, Steve? But where you're going now, I guess you'll have to go it alone."

"That's not my name," I said.

"It's a sad thing, death," said William. "I can't think of anything sadder. It really fills me up with a melancholy feeling when I think about it. But what you're doing, Steve, what you're giving us, this gift that you're giving us by letting us share these last days with you, this gift is immeasurable, Steve, priceless, it's the Hope Diamond of gifts, the crown jewels of enriching spiritual experiences, like a Lamborghini with all the trimmings, or a house and real acreage in Malibu, and I mean beachfront, a big sturdy house, too, not one of those wash-away, mudslide shitboxes, I'm talking about something built with fucking care, but anyway, that doesn't matter, that's not my point, because the thing is, the thing of it is, Steve, those things, all of those material objects, they have prices, so how could they compare to your goddamn priceless gift that transcends material realms? How could they ever compare to this gift you've bestowed upon all of us here in what is essentially my home but is also, on some deeper spiritual level, your home, too, by dint of you opening your heart to us and allowing us all into your last desperate moments so that you, too, belong as much as I do to what is essentially my house where I have essentially financed all of the comforts you deserve in this last, terrible waning of your life, comforts financed, I should add, with no ponying up by certain nameless cheapskates, though I might mention there were intimations of some kind of contribution from these unnamed nickel-pinching parties, parties who have already profited from your affliction, which is all just to say, really, that my outlay, and I mean my emotional as well as financial outlay, because of the situation here, the situation vis-à-vis Maryse, not to mention the situation vis-à-vis Fiona, this lovely girl, this lovely girl-woman with whom, and I don't mean to hurt you, Steve, in fact I hope it helps in its way, eases your transit, as it were, with whom I've developed something of a paternal bond with, though not forgetting for a moment my emotions as they vis-à-vis you, too, Steve, which is just to say this outlay has its emotional as well as financial aspects—bed, board, medicine, laundry, all the things, in fact, one associates with a well-tended send-off, a lavish bon voyage, a top-shelf sayonara—nonetheless it's an outlay, that, even in toto, in financial and emotional toto, cannot begin to compare with what you've given us, Steve, the gift of witness, here at the end of the ballgame, here at the end of the so-called road, here at the terminus of terminal, where every twitch and murmur of your up-till-now, every dream you've ever dreamed, every sensation you've ever, well, sensated, waves goodbye like doomed doughboys on a troopship. Once more, I must reiterate, how could anything compare to such a gift? Forget my outlay, the Lamborghini, the beachfront joint with crackerjack ground work, or that big rock so many historically oppressed, oxygen-deprived Africans died prying loose, what could rival your gift, Steve, this revelatory, keeps-on-giving gift, wherein you offer up your life to make our lives that much more meaningful, that much more, well, lived. So, to you, I raise, or rather, now, extend, my glass, my love, my gratitude. Thank you, Steve, thank you."

"Thank *you*, William," said Maryse.

"Shit," said William, "was the camera on?"

"The light's lit," said Fiona.

"Let's feast."

"Fuck it," I said.

"What, Steve?" said Maryse. "The roast? It's a lovely roast."

"Not the roast," I said.

"Fuck what, Daddy?" said my daughter.

"Scandinavia," I said.

. . .

I decided not to die. Not here, not now. I knew my number was nearing up, but my fettle was nearly fine again. Conundrum? Contradiction? Contraindication? Probably the Philosopher would have sneered it away. Mere remission, he'd have said, malady's lull, death catching its breath, a little pre-crossing picnic by the Styx.

Probably he'd be right.

I got up, cased the joint, cat-burgled around, searched and seized. Jewelry, cash, checkbooks, credit cards. The gold rope I gave Maryse one anniversary. The gold earrings I gave her another. Money from all the places I supposed a typical William to keep it—cookie jars, cigar boxes, smuggler's almanacs, antique licorice tins. I scooped up wallets, keys, coins. I rolled William's convertible out of the driveway, gave myself a swift lecture in stick.

"I am me," I said, aimed for the interstate.

Items #7

I drove to Cudahy's grave. Cudahy had no grave. I parked and walked the pathways of the tony boneyard where somewhere a sandwich-sized wedge of granite bore his name. We'd cindered him, after all, old Cudahy, poured him into the Florentine— where were his ashes now? In mini-storage? On a hock shop shelf? Beside the chipped china and warped seventy-eights at some old biddy's going-out-of-subsistence yard sale?—but an anonymous donor had sprung for a marker, a simple stone in this spare outer lawn, this necropolitan burb, set aside for the absentee dead.

We'd never discovered the name of the donor. We'd never

bothered. Who didn't have the distant dowager aunt some-where, the rumored relation, the cash uncle who'd let you dan-gle in your day-to-day but who could be counted on to shout for the quality engravature that pronounced your finitude?

I didn't, actually, but we'd all concluded Cudahy did. We'd blown his wad on the big vase, so who else?

Now I walked these stone rows, bent here and there for the stenciled calendrics of Cudahy. I had something to say to him, maybe, or something to say in the vicinity of his granite men-tion. I walked beneath a low mean sky that somehow made the long lawn lusher. Like it had secret sun in it, a spy for bright-ness, a sunshine mole. It was deep swollen light, the kind that hung over us that boyhood day we stood beneath the toolshed window, Cudahy and I, propping each other up on a cinder block to peep.

It was our fathers, Cudahy's father, my father, that toolshed not big enough for the one father, let alone two, no room at all in there, really, rake tines porcupined out of barrels, leaf-blow-ers resting on tarp heaps, hoes, spades, tool chests, bait boxes, cartons of nuts, of bolts, of screws and gears and nails, the weekend handyman's arsenal, his ammo dump, all manner of thingamabob there in casual stockpilage in that dank, mouse-turded dark.

It was all of this and our fathers, fuming.

Because of the mower blade. Because Cudahy's father had borrowed my father's lawn mower and the blade was cracked where maybe it hadn't been cracked before.

I knew all about it. Who didn't at our dinner table? Listen past the clatter of casserole lids and you will never wonder later what murdered your kin. They tell you straight off. They bear you to bear witness. It was the mower blade, the crisis to usurp all crises, and never at a better time, either, the kind of catastrophe that spelled instant amnesia for all the nagging failures of my father's current administration—the unpaid gas bill, the unscooped rain gutters—or even my misdeeds, my messy room, my algebraic woes, my budding notoriety as a tree-torcher, a whiskey thief. The mower blade had buried all the local news. It wasn't a domestic issue, not even a border dispute. It was an international incident.

So here were our fathers, fuming. Our fathers, who'd never dared to like each other anyway, Mr. Cudahy, the buzzcut vet, the grizzled Mama Bell lineman, always with his big, beautiful laugh and those special clips for scaling pole rungs hanging from his belt like some alloyed adjunct to virility—those clips were maybe for scaling tall women, too—and that huge orange lineman's telephone for plugging in anywhere, for listening, for listening in, to his barber, his banker, his boss, to anybody he pleased, to strangers, to housewives, to horny teens, to seditious profs at the community college, or for calling, calling his bookie, calling his chippy, calling home, him clipped to a pole in a rainstorm and wondering what's for dinner—"How about you with a cherry on top, honey?"—for calling in airstrike, death from above, for calling the mayor, the president, or Captain Thornfield, even, for calling in his markers, his favors, his slips, for calling the play, for calling the shots, for calling all of them *out*, and my father, the Frigidaire elegist, the seawall dreamer, an island of a man whipped by inner monsoon, not a broken man but maybe too much bent, caught in some crooked, voluptuous glide through that no-fly zone between the forestalled and the forsook, my father maybe somehow forging for himself a power in hating this Cudahy, this swaggering, cackling, doubtless Cudahy, a power in caring enough to hate, that soulforce summoned from having a stake in a wager all the fiercer for being finally prizeless—the money, the women, the kicks long paid out, the teller gone, the bank broke—and Mr. Cudahy, Mr. Cudahy maybe never giving my father much thought in the first place, but, if pushed, knowing it was best to hate the crud back, maybe just for being one of the ground-dwellers, one of the surface saps (no rung-buffed boots, no climbing clips, no field phone, no bookie, no nookie), one of the puny, the ant-people, some bitter simp who couldn't be neighborly if he tried, couldn't neighbor his way out of a paper bag, who makes a federal case out of a freaking mower blade, who drags a fine man into a stinking shed to bitch about an old crack in some rusted-to-shit excuse for a lawn maintenance machine, drags *him*, of all people, drags Cudahy, a near-hero hereabouts, the closest thing to mythic in the township, who toils daily between earth and sky, who is decent and neighborly always, a ladder-lender, a driveway-waver, or if the jerk needs a jump, and not because he gives one shit for the guy, either, not because of anything like that.

Hell, no.

Because of the sons. Because of the friendship of their sons. Because that is something to respect, to value, to fend for (even if the toaster poet doesn't get it, could never even comprehend), because whatever is between these boys deserves to be shielded from ant bitterness, from town pain, because that's it, that's all you get in the end, a friend, one if you're lucky, one who doesn't catch a sapper's bullet in freaking Korea (if you're lucky), one who doesn't wrap his jalopy around an oak trunk (if you're lucky), one who doesn't botch a lifetime of I've-Got-Your-Back with a tipsy grope at the wife (if you're lucky), and who of us is ever truly lucky?

Because of the boys, the sons, who even now were on tippy-toes under the toolshed window, straining for a peep.

"So," we heard my father say, "I guess the rocks really needed some trimming, huh? Figured the yard's all done, might as well mow the rocks while I still have the guy's machine."

"Look, I didn't mow no rocks, Charlie," said Mr. Cudahy. "I'm sorry."

"What are you sorry for? You said you didn't mow any rocks. Or *no* rocks, rather."

This last was so shameless, so shameful, the fop's swipe, the nerd's gnaw, so laced with the venom of soft men, that I looked to my friend there beneath the sill, beseeched forgiveness, but I don't think Boy Cudahy even caught the slight to his father's speech, or maybe he had, of course he had, it just wasn't the terrible rent in his world I thought it to be, or that maybe my father intended. I saw it a dirk sunk to hilt in the meat of decency, equality, common cause. But to a Cudahy it probably had the same power "four-eyes" would to my bifocaled father. Big whoop. Specs. What else you got?

"I guess," said Mr. Cudahy, his voice going taut now, like cable, like strung bundle, "I guess I'm sorry the mower was broken before you gave it to me."

"Loaned."

"What?"

"I loaned the mower to you."

"Yes, Professor."

"Well, it wasn't so broken you weren't able to mow some rocks with it, now was it?"

"I told you, I didn't mow no goddamn fucking rocks!"

"Don't you dare swear in my shed."

"This was Walt Wilmer's shed before you even moved here. I helped him build the fucking thing."

"It's my shed now."

"Walt Wilmer."

"Nuts to Walt Wilmer."

"Walt Wilmer was a good man. He died protecting this community."

"He was a drunken traffic cop. His wife ran him over."

"He was protecting this community."

"I don't know what that means."

"Sure you do, Jewboy."

"You just stepped over the fucking line, Cudahy."

"Hey, don't swear in the shed, kike!"

It didn't sound like a fight. It sounded like an accident, or some vaudeville routine. I pictured our fathers in checkered suits, pratfalling in tandem, dumb grins footlight-lit.

"Hey, Jimbo, what do you know, is this a hole in the road?"

"Don't see no hole, Charlie, I think it's just fresh paiiiii-int . . ."

Then it sounded like something else was in there with them, something maybe fanged and rabid fettered to the tool-shed floor. We heard banging, bashing, what must have been the rake barrel spinning, all those wingnuts and washers and quarter-inch screws spilled out like some dragon hoard of home improvement, all those thingamabobs sliding, wheeling, rolling into thingamajigs, flipping them, flying them, and underneath it now a new noise, a slow, pressured thrashing, as though our fathers were vying for great gruesome grips on the floor, for spine-snapping holds, full and infernal Nelsons, each man sliding, straining, torquing for purchase, for a death blow, even, but it never came. There was only a thud and then another thud, hard breathing, moans.

Cudahy cupped his hands under the window and I slipped in my Ked for a hoist. I caught sight of them before his fingers—not yet the cannonball shovers they would someday become—gave way. Our fathers were shored up together against the wall planks, eyes shut, shirts torn, knuckles torn, blood riding eddies of sweat down their cheeks. They looked like a famous photograph of war, some newsweekly pin-up of noble woe. They rubbed their arms, tested their necks, bit down on pulped lips.

"Who won?" whispered Cudahy.

Cudahy hadn't seen what I'd seen. For him it was still my-father-can-beat-up-your-father, understandable, really, part of the protocol, in fact, but my vision of them there together in that ruined place—everything upturned, upended, all order murdered, the floor studded with oddments, the rakes and spades and hoes heaped like some peasant rebellion's surrender—had changed everything. These were new men now.

We'd have to be new boys.

"Nobody won," I said.

"What do you mean nobody won?"

"Shh," I said.

We heard them through the shed wood.

"Jesus, Jim," said my father. "I'm sorry."

"Didn't know you had it in you, Charlie."

"Jesus, Jim."

"Haven't banged around like that in a while."

"My first fight."

"No shit? You did good, Charlie. You're a maniac."

"I thought I was a pacifist. Against the war, you know."

"Hell, the war was bullshit."

"We're all animals, Jim."

"Take it easy, buddy. You weren't that good. I could have kicked your ass if it came down to it. Still might."

"You're a big man, Jim. Big Jim."

"Big Jim Cudahy. Big everywhere. Big where it counts."

"Sure you are."

"No shit. Ask your wife."

"I did."

"Fuck."

"It's all right, Jim."

"Shit. What'd she say. Oh, fuck."

"Forget about it, Jim."

"Just like that?"

"Just like that."

"You're a better man than I am, Charlie."

"Clearly I'm not. So, let's see it."

"What?"

"Let's see it."

"Whoa, there, buddy."

"No, really, let's see Big Jim's big 'un."

"Now I'm really going to have to beat the crap out of you."

"Want to see mine?"

"What the hell?"

"No, really."

"Really?"

"Really."

"You, too, then."

"Me, too, then."

"You won't be sorry."

"I'm always sorry."

We listened for a while, a shuffle of boots, buttons unsnapping. We listened and heard nothing. Then we heard something. It didn't mean anything, really. It was a couple of men finding some kind of solace in darkness, I guess. It was a couple of men with nothing in common but four hands and two cocks between them.

I looked over at Cudahy.

We'd have to be better friends than we'd ever been or no friends at all.

"Somebody won," said Cudahy.

"No," I said, "it was a draw."

Now I walked the cemetery grounds, poked around for Cudahy's stone. Near some weeds I spotted a granite sarcophagus that said Kippelman. I laid some nylon roses on it. Cudahy had been a great believer in fake flowers, fake teeth, fake fur.

"Everything God makes rots," he'd said.

I laid a card down beside the roses.

"Kippelman," I wrote. "Please hold for Cudahy."

I drove west, took a room in the hills, the Landview Inn Motel.

"We used to be an inn, in the olden days," said the woman who'd risen from a plate of sauerkraut when I'd tapped the bell. "We're a motel now, but we enjoy the historical significance of our past. Aaron Burr bedded a lady here. How long are you staying?"

"I don't know."

"That's not a problem."

"I'll have a better answer tomorrow."

"Tomorrow's the big day, huh?"

"What do you mean?"

"Tomorrow the cows come home."

"I don't follow."

"I didn't ask you to follow," said the woman. "I'm sorry. I don't know what's wrong with me. I guess I'm not in a welcoming mood. I'm pooped. People think motel people just sit on their butts and pass out keys. There's a lot more to it."

"I don't doubt it."

"That's kind of you not to doubt it," the woman said, looked at my credit card. "William."

"Bill."

"I'm Fran. Fran Kincaid."

"You're kidding."

"It's not a very funny name, Bill, why would I be kidding? I mean Fran's sort of funny, like Gertrude, or something. I'll grant you that. But Kincaid? I like the sound of Kincaid. Hearty, right? I knew a guy named Murray Murray. Now that's funny. Jewish fellow. Not that I care. Happened to be Hebrew. We kissed, that's all. Not because of the Jew thing. I'm attracted to Jews. Einstein stayed here with his mistress in the fifties. Not that he was attractive. But you figure a guy who knows how the universe works would probably have a knack for smaller-scale manipulations, too, if you get my meaning. I'm sure you get my meaning. You seem like a worldly man of the world, William."

"Bill."

"I like William better. Do you mind if I call you William? It sounds more historical."

"Tell me, Fran, have you worked here long?"

"All my life. Or, well, a while. A few years."

"I once knew a Fran Kincaid. We were pen pals."

"Were you in prison?"

"No."

"Because a lot of gals write to cons. It's good to know where your man is every night. Oh, wait, I've heard of this. *She* was in prison."

"Nobody was in prison."

"Well, William, I never wrote you when you were in the slam. Seeing you now, I'm kind of sorry I didn't."

"Can I have my key?"

"Here. Don't worry, I've got a set, too."

I picked up a pint of rye at a package store across the interstate. My hunt for a complimentary Landview Inn Motel water glass proved futile and I had to make do with Dixie cups. This wasn't a bad thing, though I find it pretty hard to drink from a Dixie cup without tasting toothpaste. Someday there will be surgical remedy for this sort of thing. I called directory assistance and asked for my father's telephone number.

"Does your father have a name?"

"Oh, right," I said.

The old man let it ring for a while.

"Dad."

"My boy."

"That's me. How're the nibs?"

"I'm about to strike a deal for a Hink's Civic Stainless. Maybe a Mitchell's Fairie, too, although this Kraut down in Brownsville is playing tough guy. The nib world is no place for the gentle, kid. But you've got to do what you've got to do. You can't worry too much if you're righteous. You've got to give it up to the qelippah sometimes."

"The what?"

"The power of evil, son. It's a Kabbala thing, you wouldn't understand."

"Dad, you're really deep in this stuff."

"I've been deep in all my life. I'm clawing my way out now. So when do I get to see my boy?"

"Well, I'm actually near you. I thought I'd—"

"This is a really bad time for me, kid. I'm closing in on that Hinks. Winnie's real busy, the kids are around, court-mandated house arrest, you know. Menachem's LoJack is too tight and we've got to get *that* dealt with."

"It's okay, Dad."

"Next time you swing through Pittsburgh. How are you, though? Good?"

"Not good."

"Good. I was worried about you. I saw you on TV and all that. Then I didn't hear from you. I respected your decision not to involve me. I probably would have complicated things anyway. But it sounds like you're all better now. I'm happy about that. No father wants to see his son die. Not before a reasonable age. That's just the way of nature. I'll call you soon. Or you call me. When this Hinks thing, when it's in the can. Isn't that what you Hollywood people say?"

"I was never in Hollywood, Dad."

"This is the big one. I thought the Brandauer was the big one but that was before the Hinks."

"Good luck."

"I don't need luck. I have faith."

"Fuckeroo'd," I said.

"Excuse me?"

. . .

The TV was bolted to the wall near the ceiling. There was no remote. I had to hop up on the bureau to work the dials. Was this how Einstein did it? Maybe he made his mistress change the channels. Not that they had much to choose from in those days. Puppets, mostly, maybe a Senate hearing. Probably just wanted to see up her poon, Einstein. He was pretty damn old by then. Maybe even dead.

High up on the dial, past all the softcore sumo and night hunts of the snow owl, was a show I'd never seen before. *The Realms,* it was called, or at least those were the words that pulsed continuously in the corner of the screen. Sometimes there was a graphic, too, a sketch of a thatch-roofed hut. The whole thing was hard to follow, all dissolves and bleeds and wipes. Nude people drifted in and out of mostly empty rooms. Sometimes the rooms had chairs in them, or a ceiling fan, or a pail of soapy water. One room was knee-high with topsoil. A man in buckskin and a ski mask stabbed at the dirt with a shovel, let the blade scrape concrete. Now two women cuddled in a hammock, talked in low grave tones.

"Woodland apes," said one.

"Spawn of," said another.

She pointed across the room to where a man stood eating some whitish substance from a peel-off container. It took me a while to place him. The bones in his face had slid around a bit, the skin was bumpier, seamed.

But it was absolutely Bobby Trubate.

"Guess you're wondering what the hell is going on," he said now to the camera. "Let me explain something about the Realms. The Realms is the Realms. My new friend Warren said that. I couldn't agree more. The only thing I'd add is that the Realms is the Realms is the Realms. It's where we all truly live. It's not fantasy. It's not reality. It's not another world. It's not television, though you're certainly welcome to tune in. It's not the Internet, though I think you're lost if you're not already a part of our online community. It's not a movement. We hardly move at all. It's not a paradox, but it's guaranteed to blow your mind. It's not even a business, though we do accept all major credit cards. Would you like to see something? I'd like you to see something."

He led the camera through a door into a narrow room. There was a hospital bed, a bony old man up to his ribs in sheet. The walls were a trompe l'oeil of desert dunes and sky. The trick didn't quite take. You could see where the paint got grainy, the streaks of charcoal underneath. The old man sat up in bed. His hair was patched and stiff, his arms spindly, his skin stippled with rot.

"Good morning, evening," Trubate said to him softly.

"Good afternoon," said Heinrich.

Now the screen went white. The rest of the evening's local cable line-up started to scroll. Something called *Landview Today* was on next. Sallow men in varsity satin argued the merits of a new turnpike toll. I tugged a fresh Dixie cup from the stack, grateful for such distraction after the shock of seeing Heinrich. Christ, how long had it been? How long in Pangburn Falls? How long in the guilt room? How long in the Landview Inn Motel? It feels of an evening with your Dixie cups, your rye. It could be years. Carthage gets covered with Tunisian condos, or moves to Tennessee.

How long had Heinrich known he was sick?

"Time has never lost in overtime," he'd told me once.

Whatever was having at him now was no mystery plague, either. It looked like a good old fashioned tumor party, cell bullies pulling the body dirtward. I stared at the TV, tried to focus on the Landview spat, blot Heinrich out. I was listing toward support of the toll hike when the liquor put me under.

Near dawn there was a noise at the door. Some carouser in the wrong keyhole, I figured, a demo-kit pilgrim back from a sports bar score.

"Who's there?"

The lock clicked and Fran Kincaid walked in, kicked off her shoes. She had a maid's apron on.

"Do you want me to wear this?" she said.

"Don't you own the place?"

"This is fantasy time."

"It's a little late," I said. "Or a little early."

"I had to finish the books. I promised my husband I'd get the books done. Now do you want busty mature woman sex or not?"

"Sure," I said.

"No mommy tit shit. We're beasts of the field, okay?"

"Okay."

Fran was no stranger to the field. When we were finished I watched her shimmy back into her jeans, fix her hair in the mirror as though trying to approximate the wife her husband had last seen, the bitch who hadn't done the books yet. I could smell bad hubby a mile away. It smelled like me. She balled up the apron and stuffed it in her pocket.

"Did you enjoy yourself, William?"

"I did," I said. "But I still can't get over the fact that your name is Fran Kincaid."

"It's the doppelgänger effect, I guess."

"Something like that," I said.

"You really miss her, don't you?"

"Who?"

"Stop lying to yourself, William. You are you, and that's all there is to it. You just need a little continuum awareness, is all."

"The Realms," I said.

"I couldn't watch last night," said Fran. "I told you, I was doing the books. But my husband tapes them all. That Bobby Trubate is a dreamcake. Now, William, it's time for me to say good morning, evening. I've got a lot of work to do. As you may have noticed, I don't just sit on my butt all day. Checkout's eleven-thirty."

I checked out around ten, bought some gas, got back on the highway heading west. I'd never seen the heart of the country. I figured it all for corporate parks and sick prairie grass. Apparently there were also some malls. I pulled off into one in Ohio, bought a knockwurst sandwich and a bag of chips—"flavored with other natural flavors"—sat on a wrought-iron bench in the middle of a freezing atrium. The coffee shop across the way had a brick facade and ornate signage much like that used in commercials to convey the supposed muffin-consciousness of Industrial England. A big blond cop walked out with some kind of roll in his hand. He put his boot on the bench.

"Yum," said the cop. "Mocha bagel."

"I got knockwurst," I said.

"Get it with golden mustard?"

"I did."

"Smart move."

"Thank you."

"You're not from around here, are you? I can tell by your mannerisms. You use your hands a lot."

"I'm eating."

"Can I ask you something?"

"Sure."

"What do you think of cops?"

"Cops," I said.

"I want to write a TV show about a cop and another guy. The cop part is easy, but the other guy, what he thinks about the cop, I need to do research. So I'm asking all the smart people I meet what they think about cops."

"Why do I qualify as smart?"

"The mustard. Your mannerisms."

"Who's the other guy?" I said.

"He's this guy. He's not a cop. It's becoming a real pain in the neck. I'm blocking on the non-cop mentality. Can't you give me something?"

"Cops have guns," I said.

"That's it. That's all I needed. I knew you were the guy to ask. Fare thee well, me. Good afternoon, breakfast."

"Excuse me?"

"I'm just beginning to pick up the lingo."

"I should get going," I said.

I got some news on the radio. The oldest man in the world had just admitted to lying about his age. "I feel bad about it," said Willett Phillips, fifty-three, "but the yogurt people dangled a lot of cash in front of me." Harvard seniors were gearing up for an international event they'd organized for credit, A Day Without Exploitation. The CEOs of several major corporations had already pledged to pay overseas factory workers minimum wage for the day. Some American-based companies had promised full health benefits for the twenty-four-hour period. "If I'm going to lose my arm," said Glen French of Flint, Michigan, "I pray it's on Tuesday." Speeches and a concert were planned. In other news, the third unclaimed nuclear device in as many weeks had been detonated over the Pacific, this time in the vicinity of the Cook Islands. When asked to comment, a spokesman for the State Department said, "Somebody's having some fun." Meanwhile, advertisers were lining up to air spots on *The Realms*, the runaway underground multimedia hit to be pancast by several networks and content companies at once. Said *Realms* creator and host Bobby Trubate from his headquarters in Death Valley, "We'd do this for free, but we wouldn't. The main thing, though, is to win people over to the idea of spirit-based branding. We're a spiritual delivery system. People are tired of reality, and they're too smart for fantasy. It was just a matter of time before somebody figured out what was next. This is the marketplace of ideals, and we mean to corner it. *The Realms* is just the tip of the ice pick. I want our advertisers to know that. The dream of the wireless Xanadu is alive. I'm literally on the verge of decreeing stately pleasure domes, here, people."

I hit the tuning scanner, found some old-time Muzak. It was the purest, truest thing I'd heard in a while. I pictured the viola section in loose-fitting Hawaiian shirts, listened to them ride the chordal swell. They were doing a rendition of something once regarded by rock magazine capsule reviewers as cruelly melodic and teeming with surplus malaise. These fiddle boys were bowing such sweetness back into it. I wept on past the Ohio state line.

The question of why William's credit card was still valid tender continued to gnaw when I heard the birdsounds in the glove box. Glad chirp of sparrow on a microchip. I dug around for the phone, found it, flipped it.

"Go," I said.

Goddamn, it was good to say that.

I got the buzz of bad frequency, a harried satellite.

"Hello?" I said. "William?"

"It's Bobby. Can you hear me?"

"In and out."

"Good . . ."

"I missed that."

"Now?"

"Yeah."

"How do you like Indiana?"

"Are you tracking me?"

"Drama queen."

"What happened to the freedom of the open road?"

"You're free to stop at any roadside concession. There's a Stuckey's coming up. I recommend the candied almond log."

"Is that my password?"

"No, it's just totally tasty."

The redemption van crapped black smoke in the Stuckey's parking lot. I pulled William's convertible up beside it, got out. The van door slid open and Dietz smiled down. His ponytail was tucked inside his derby. The loop hung down like a silky noose.

"Brother in fire," said Dietz, giggling. "Welcome to the whirligig."

"I've got a ride," I said. "But thanks."

"I don't think you're going to get too far," said a voice behind me. It was Old Gold. He was tearing up packets of diner sugar, pouring them into William's gas tank. Dietz grabbed me by the arms. His grip was tremendous. We had to wait for Old Gold to tear up all the packets, dig for more in his pants.

"I told you we should have gotten the fucking box," said Dietz. "Eighty-nine cents."

"That's a rip-off," said Old Gold.

"We expense it."

"Then we have to explain it."

"Just cut the tires."

"Radials," said Old Gold. "Bad for the knife."

Old Gold drove. Dietz sat in back with me. There was a shovel there, the bed of it shiny, the blade edge blacked with oil. Dietz picked it up, poked at some bright netting torn loose from clementine crates.

"My mother used to wear ones like these," he said. "Slut hose."

"No more boat," I said.

"There's always more boat."

"Shut up back there," said Old Gold. "Dietz, did you drop those tabs? That's all I need. I'm commander of this operation."

"What, nobody ever did a magic dance on your Navy SEAL Team?"

"I wasn't no SEAL," said Old Gold. "I was an intelligence."

Dietz fell back laughing, hugged the shovel blade.

"Good stuff, Dietz?" I said. "See anything special?"

"I don't have visions anymore, man. Too many golden fucking arches obstructing the view. Lookie there. Death burgers on both sides of the road. Motherfuckers get you coming and going."

"It's your peers that are responsible, Dietz," I said. "They made this world."

I pointed out the window to the world.

"My peers? My peers been dead since '73. Don't lay that trip on me, man. Those people you're talking about, they were pigs all along. Pigs with beards, pigs on skag, little sows with blond hair down to their asses and sweet little piggy tits. Must I give you a lesson in cultural . . . cultural . . . oh, shit . . ."

Dietz began to wriggle, beetle-like, batted his arms in the air.

"Good morning, evening!" he said.

"Don't mock the rituals," snarled Old Gold. "It's bad karma."

"Karma?" said Dietz. "You moron. Hey, pull over. Let's get a burger. They make them with fetus meat now."

"Can it, Dietz," said Old Gold. "Or I'm going to do something evil."

"Evil?" said Dietz. "You don't have the sensitivity for evil. All you're capable of is mean. Man, if Heinrich was still Heinrich he'd show you a thing about—"

"I said can it," said Old Gold.

"Indiana," said Dietz, after a while, as though it might be a disputed philosophical supposition.

"This here is downstate Illinois," said Old Gold. "They

have signs about it for people like you who can't tell the difference."

"Mind if I ask you guys a question?" I said.

"Mind," said Dietz. "How many times do you think I've said the word mind?"

"Where are you taking me?" I said.

"To your rightful place," said Old Gold.

We took a turnoff, sped up a ramp. Withered fields whipped by. I looked down at the shovel, up at Dietz. I wondered if I'd have to dig my own grave like some mob saga hood. I could storyboard the whole thing if they wanted.

"Turn here," said Dietz.

I peered out the window for a peek at my last location, but the only sights I saw were airport signs, a tinted tower by a pond.

Items #8

We flew out on a cheapo line, Phaethon Air. Dietz flourished tickets and we charged through the gate. Old Gold drove off with the van. Phaethon security was a coke-shaky clubkid with a billy bat. He wanted to know if we'd left anything unattended in the terminal.

"Just my detonator," said Dietz.

The kid laughed, waved us through.

"Realm it up!" he called.

"I use Phaethon for most of my travel. They're fans."

We boarded, found our seats. We'd been assigned to something called urbane class. There was little in the way of leg room and no magazines, just old foreign affairs journals, some soft sculpture catalogues. The pipe racks fitted in the seatbacks were filled with posies and incense sticks. Stuffed in the pocket webbing, alongside some sick bags, were blank diaries with embossed covers that read: *Reflections Aloft*. The inflight movie, according to a typed index card, would be a series of experimental shorts produced at McGill University in the seventies.

"What I love about this airline," said Dietz, "is that they know their niche and they work it."

The pilot's voice came over the speaker to announce we'd be taking off shortly.

"I'm feeling good about the whole takeoff thing right now," he added. "I mean, why not? Pilot error is all in the head."

A steward came by with hot towels and vodka shots.

Dietz lit up an enormous spliff.

"I'm sorry, sir," said the steward, "you can't smoke that in here."

Dietz winked a bloodshot eye, gave the guy a hit.

I looked around for signs of censure but nobody seemed to notice. There were about a dozen people on board. Some were in leather and all were asleep.

"Kiwis," said Dietz. "Crazy motherfuckers."

"What's their niche?" I said.

"Okay," said Dietz. "I lied to you. This isn't really an airline. But you'll thank me when you taste the lemon chicken."

I spotted a few more passengers under blankets in the back of the plane, tiptoed past them to the bathrooms. The lock plate in one of the doors said Need. The other said Want. I went for Want. The door whacked up on a pair of knees.

"Sorry," I said.

"Come in."

I slid through the door, leaned up on the sink.

"Dropping some friends off at the lake," said the Rad Balm girl.

"So, you wanted company?"

"I didn't know it was you, fuckstick."

"Right."

The exit was a bit trickier, requiring a sort of high hurdle kick to clear. I leaned on Need. Need was not occupado. I locked myself in, sat down. The pilot's voice crackled over the intercom.

"Steve, you're all flustered. Over."

"My name's not Steve," I said.

"It's so tiring, your denial. Over."

"Your voice is really crackling," I said. "Over."

We touched down a few hours later. I looked out the window as we made our approach, saw blasted earth and cracked desert roads looping into emptiness. I didn't see any airport. Dietz had nodded off next to me, spliff stub poking cold from his knuckles. Some of the leather men were playing hacky sack in the aisle, shouting in strange English. Something about a wingeing sod off his tits in Auckland, a bunch of silly cunts. The pilot announced that he'd lowered the landing gear, requested that we please refrain from dread. I shook Dietz awake.

"Where the fuck are we?"

"We're in the land of dreams. Sunny California. Hollywood, to be exact."

"This is the desert," I said.

"Mulholland Drive," said Dietz. "Sunset and Vine. Betty Grable. Fatty Arbuckle. Bad fatty. Hollywood Walk of Fame.

A star for Steve. A star for Dietz. We'll marry Brazilian models. We'll battle addiction."

"This is the desert," I said. "This isn't even the desert where people go and say, Oh, I went to the desert, I lost eighty bucks on the slots but I found this skull. This is actually the fucking desert."

"Okay," said Dietz, "I lied to you. It's the desert."

We had to wait for the emergency chutes to inflate. Dietz said the deplaning platform was on the fritz. The New Zealanders were having chicken fights in the rear of the cabin. A great cheer went up as one man split his head on the luggage bin.

Layover fever, Dietz said.

We slid down to the desert floor, walked out across the waste. We walked for a while. The Rad Balm girl and some of her friends were with us, a few of the New Zealanders, too. There were some kids in skate pads who said they were from St. Louis. The going was slow. Every few feet there was a blindside tackle, a tussle in the sand. The man who'd injured himself on the luggage bin was beaten severely again. His mates laughed and called him a poof. The skate kids spit on his head. It appeared he'd been sacrificed by the Kiwis to the greater glory of international goodwill.

"Violence will be met with decisive violence," said Dietz, but nobody paid him any heed.

We passed the remnants of an encampment. Empty water bottles, tattered tents. Sun-browned business cards lay strewn with charred bones in a fire pit. There was a jar of glitter on a rock, a cell phone wedged in the crook of a cactus. Signs and pseudo-signs. Sense and sensimilla. Goofball shit.

"Thought they were the new Dionysians," said Dietz. "They're all dead now."

"They're not dead," I said. "They got downsized."

"You tell your story, I'll tell mine."

Just past the next rise we caught sight of a huge metal-skinned hangar. It could have been the hull of some alien ship, sunk belly up in ancient sea boil. More likely it was something the feds had pawned off in the last budget crisis, or forgotten about entirely, abandoned to the war nerds who sneaked inside to jot maps, jack soda machines.

The glare off the hangar was strong. Dietz handed me a pair of aviator glasses. As I put them on I heard the plane start to taxi behind us.

"Don't look back," he said. "You'll turn into All-Spice."

"Right," I said.

"There are a lot of little shits where we're going," said Dietz. "Don't let it get to you. Remember who you are. You're the Subject Steve."

"Right," I said.

We swung down a high ridge to the hangar. Dietz called to some men lounging near the enormous door. It took them a while to slide it back. There were shapes there in the darkness, lit hives receding into the vast cool of the room. Varnished deskpieces in workstation clusters spiraled out of a raised hub. Kids, dozens of kids in bughead earphones tapped away at consoles in low golden light. There was a kind of liquid quiet in the room, a strange drone joy. People tapped each other, whispered, giggled softly over the tidal click of keypads.

Most of the workstations included a shelving unit for extra drives, office swag. Exhibits in kiddie kitsch abounded. TV tie-in lunchbox collections, Matchbox cars, bandoleer'd action figures. They seemed to be the same order of artifact my peers had hoarded, though I had only the vaguest sense of these versions. They'd probably reigned the schoolyards about the time I was blowing dormroom snowcaps with William. Dietz led me past a set of plastic poodles hanging on a wire. The dogs lit up and yapped.

"I me ma," they said. "I ma me."

We cut through a row of cube dividers to the hub area. Bobby Trubate sat with his feet up in a white leather easy chair. He wore rope sandals, a mesh robe with platinum trim, the outfit of a man who goes to court to have his name changed to a prime number. Bits of the mesh were dark with sweat. He flipped his ring binder shut.

"Steve-o. Get up here, buddy!"

He hoisted me up to his dais, bent me in a tender headlock.

"Nice place," I said, ducked loose from his robe folds.

"Should of seen this dump before I leased it. Brought in the best industrial decorator around. My investors went nuts, but fuck them. They invested in a visionary so they should expect vision. Dietz, you old fuck, hold the fort."

I followed Trubate through a side door into a wide wood-beamed room. It was skylit, full of lush rustic comforts, animal skins, teak. A bank of monitors was mounted in the wall. Some screens showed Realms locations, the soil room, the hospital bed. Others scrolled pages from the Realms website, or sur-veilled the workers in the hangar. A few pulled in random pro-gramming, soccer games from South America, Polish soaps. The thatch hut logo blinked from every corner.

"Can I get you something?" said Trubate. "Vodka frappé? A frosty rail?"

"Is that the road to redemption?"

"Things have changed a bit."

"They seemed to have changed a lot for Heinrich," I said.

"Unless it's your makeup team that's made him look like death."

"No," he said, "that's death."

Trubate squinnied his eyes. There was something scooped-out about him, I saw now, sick. A thin vein in his temple was thumping hard. I wondered what dregs of goodies it was bearing from his brain.

"I don't know," he said softly. "It's so fucked. I almost feel like it's my fault. He wasn't strong enough for the relocation. The tumors moved fast."

"So did you."

"The hut did some shit to me," he said. "Maybe not what Heinrich had in mind. The branks. The breast ripper. I saw it all so plain after that. I'd been such a child. They say actors are children."

"So you wanted to direct."

"Don't be snide. Snidery is the last refuge of dickwads. The Center was no longer viable. It was time to take things to the next level. I couldn't run away from my talent. I *am* Hollywood, after all. I am more than Hollywood."

"Old Gold, too?"

"Hey, everyone was welcome. Heinrich was *sick*. The bills were piling up. The marshals were coming. I made some phone calls. Saved the fucking day. We have a new home for you, Steve. But you've got to earn your keep."

Trubate batted something out of my hair.

"Ladybug," he said.

"Let's see it."

"Maybe not a ladybug," said Trubate, pinched something in his fingers to a smear. "I've got to scram. Goddamn investor teleconference. They don't like the figures. Fuck the figures.

They want their money. Fuck them. Do I look like I have the money? If I'd spent it on speedballs and pussy they'd understand. That they can get their heads around. But a glimpse of the truth? No fucking way."

Trubate cut loose with a cackle.

"I'm working on the cackle," he said.

I milled around the room, inspected the mail-order baubles. There appeared to be some sort of nautical motif in effect, solid gold sextants, diving bells that doubled as ice buckets, stereo speakers mounted in the galleon wood. A lot of it looked culled from those old magazines at the Center, Estelle Burke's yearbooks. Don't forget the postcard from Paris. Remember me when you're a crazed futurist.

A stack of coasters on the coffee table bore the hut logo in safety orange. The Realms Is Real, they proclaimed. I found a leather binder with some hole-punched pages. It was a business plan, a pretty primitive-looking one at that, some smudged graphs, a brief budget breakdown whose figures didn't add up. One section was entitled the Trubate Brand, another the Heinrich Time-Sensitivity Factor. A list of future projects included the Daddy Chair, the Gimp Snatch Miracle Hour, and the Subject Steve. A parenthetical following this last noted that the executive producer credit had been "preguaranteed" to one Leon Goldfarb.

Now one of the monitors in the wall fired off a series of high squawks. Heinrich leaned into frame, his face puckered, papery. He lay supine on his counterpane in bikini briefs, his nipples blacked with cork. The bed was heaped with toys, baby dolls, wind-up robots, Scrabble chips.

"Hey, kids," he said. "Welcome to Heinrich's Story Bed. Looks like I'm going to tell you kids another story. Looks like all I'm good for these days is telling stories, at least according to your buddy Bobby. Bobby can't wait for me to die. Neither can I, tell you the truth. Cancer's eaten clear through me. It'll get you, too, don't worry. Meanwhile, prepare for some allegorical instruction. Do you know what that means? It means shut the fuck up and listen, because here we go. Once upon a time there was a big game hunter. This was in the time when there were big game hunters with big fucking guns and everyone understood it was a natural thing, a man versus beast thing. That's a modality that people conveniently forget these days, but it's still out there, every day, man versus beast, whether you like or not. Now this big game hunter, who happened to be from Cleveland, which is not important, but I want to make it clear he was from a highly esteemed smelting dynasty in Cleveland . . ."

There was someone else in the room. I turned and there she stood, hair up, pale arms tucked in rubber crutch locks.

"Renee."

"Look at him," she said.

"You're standing," I said. "You're walking."

"Look at the man," she said. "Saddest thing I've ever seen in my life."

"They said you'd never walk again."

"They never actually said that."

"You're walking," I said.

"Injections," she said. "Incisions. Experimental stuff. Animal cells. I have some antelope in me. Some silverback."

"Gorilla?"

"Very avant-garde. It's not the animals, though. It's the chip."

"The chip?"

"A chip in my gut. Electrodes in my legs. Bobby paid for it. Look at my crutch handles. See the buttons? I'm remote-controlling myself."

Renee twitched towards me, her crutches buzzing. Heinrich's voice careened around the room.

". . . and the hunter felt the tusk slide through him, and I'll put it bluntly, kids, the cold, sharp tusk slid through him from behind, through his anus and curving upward, just tore right through his guts and punched out his chest. Skewered, he was. Completely, irrevocably skewered. Yet even then, wriggling with the last of his life on that great bloody ivory shaft, even as the elephant lifted his head and the hunter felt the hot rank breath of the beast blanket him and its horrendous trumpet blast shatter his ears, the hunter could not understand it, and with what was left of his strength he said to the elephant, 'Why? Tell me why? You called me brother.' And the elephant blinked once and nodded, and with his trunk pushed the gored hunter to a mangled heap on the jungle floor. 'I know I called you brother,' said the elephant, shrugging his great white shoulders. 'My mistake. I must have had you mixed up with somebody else.'"

Pink pinwheels spun in Heinrich's eyes.

"Needless to say, children," he said, "Cleveland is not the manufacturing center it once was."

There were more squawks and the screen went white.

"Christ," I said.

"This is content," said Renee.

"I heard on the radio. Your big multimedia deal."

"PR bullshit. This kind of idea has been dead for a long time. We were out in the forest, what did we know? We're fucked. We're the fuckers and we're fucked."

"I've met fans."

"Like I said," said Renee.

"Renee."

"What."

"You're walking."

"This isn't really what I had in mind."

She hit the button on her crutch, just stood there, buzzing. Then she jerked away.

Everyone had gathered around Trubate's hub, a sea of wet haircuts and ghosted skin. The Rad Balm girl sat in back with a boy who'd come off the plane with us. He had lime-colored muttonchops, a denim jacket in his lap. Apparently he was getting some sort of handjob.

"Yo," I said.

"You," said the Rad Balm girl, slid her hand away.

"Get your jollies, geezer?" said the boy.

"Nice sideburns," I said. "They remind me of my father's. He was a fire captain."

"That's the most engrossing story I've ever heard."

"Better watch it," said the Rad Balm girl. "Warren's a writer, you know. That sounds so stupid. Of course you know that."

"I do now," I said.

"He's like the most famous writer in the world. The spokesman of our generation. I mean that in quotes. Spokesman in quotes. Generation, that's just generation. Whatever that means."

"Hey," said Warren. "I just do what I do. If people like it, that's cool."

"How's the fish?" I said to the Rad Balm girl.

"Fish?"

"Musician talk."

"Yeah, okay."

"Don't you remember?"

"What, do you have a photographic brain thing?"

"Excuse me?"

"Never mind."

"Okay."

"Sometimes I can't believe I actually took this job," said the Rad Balm girl. "You know, I almost went to SarinNet. That's the other big desert dot-com. They're in the silos. Package was worthless, though. Not like this is any better. People like us, we fucking made the information economy, now they're flushing us down the toilet. San Francisco, New York, Hong Kong, Brussels, Tehran, Perth, I've been pimping code all over. I just hope I can squeeze another few months out of this bullshit before everything goes bust. I know people have been saying that for years, but it's coming for real now, mark my words. What I really want to do is study medical ethics. Like what are the moral ramifications of putting a monkey head on a human body? Or a horse dick. Or like a lot of cow tits. Or is it wrong to fuck a clone of your brother if you use a rubber? That kind of crap. This place is weird, huh? The Realms. You should see some of the shit they do down there that doesn't make it past post. Bobby seems pretty creepy. What's with the robe? But I guess he has a viable business model."

"I'm sure," I said.

"Hey, you're the dying guy. You used to ball Renee, right? Somebody said that. Because Bobby's balling her now. Me, too, when I have time. I love to say ball."

"Okay."

"Just a heads-up, to use the old hippy term."

"Right," I said.

There was a man in a tight Lycra hood standing with some others near a water cooler. When the man turned to cough I saw it was the Philosopher, tricked out like some aerodynamic Franciscan. He nodded me an amen. Nearby an obese Japanese kid in a hunting vest just like Naperton used to wear was conducting impromptu Bible study with some Realms techs.

"Moses waited for the slave generation to die off," he told them. "That's why they wandered. They could have been to the Promised Land in a day. A few hours. It's like the Realms. We could expand in the snap of a finger. But if it's not the right time, our options won't be worth shit. Have you ever heard of Heinrich of Newark?"

"You mean the old freak on the bed?" said a woman with a tattoo of a water bottle on her arm.

"I mean Moses."

The kid in the vest waved off his protégés, stepped up on the dais.

"My name is Desmond Mori, Chief Personal Resources Officer, and I say to you, Good morning, morning!"

"Good afternoon," called the gathering.

The voices of the Realms were low broken things.

"Evening is upon us somewhere!" said Desmond.

"Good morning, evening."

"The past is before us!"

"We're coming, past."

"The future is gone!"

"Fare thee well, future."

"Now is . . ."

"Now."

"Now is . . ."

"Now."

"I am . . ."

"Me."

"I am . . ."

"Me."

"And who, pray tell, are you?" called Desmond, pointed over to one of the New Zealanders.

"Not a buggering bastard like you!" he said.

"I am me, me am I!" someone shouted.

"Fair dinkum?" said the New Zealander.

The woman with the water bottle tattoo punched her head against a systems panel.

"Watch my tower!" someone screamed.

"I me ma! I ma me!"

"Enough!" said Desmond, leaped from the dais, hugged the woman down to the hangar floor.

"You are you," he said, stroked her hair. "My sweet Fair Dinkum."

The room went quiet and Desmond rose with the woman in his arms, led us single file out into the sun.

"There's going to be a new policy on sick days."

Trubate stood above us on a heat-cracked mound. His mesh had stiffened with sweat. Sunlight caught the metal at his neckline. It did not make him dazzling. It looked like he was getting knifed by God.

"There will be a memo about it," he said, "but basically, no sick days."

Some hissed.

"Listen, people. We're in a tight spot right now. Forget what you hear about megadeals. That's just smoke and mirror signals. It's nothing tangible. It's nothing fungible. I'm doing everything I can for you but I need you to help yourselves. Help yourselves by working every day. All day. For us. For this. For the Realms. They want us to fail. Do you hear me? They want us to fail!"

A cheer went up and Trubate chuffed some dust with his sandal.

"I adore you all," he said. "You are my brothers and sisters. In the future they will do in-depth half-hour bios of each and every one of us. That's how important this is. Save your office party JPEGs, people! Now, I want to introduce a new family member to the Realms, the star of our latest, most innovative offering. I've known him for a long time, but it wasn't until I had a little talk with Dr. Goldfarb that we realized what a contribution he could make to our content division. So give it up for Steve!"

Nobody gave much of anything up.

Some stood and started to chat. Others found flat rocks for tanning. Desmond Mori appeared to be consoling a stick of deadwood. The St. Louis kids stalked scorpions with staple guns. Fair Dinkum scoured her head gash with sand.

We ate at long picnic benches in the back of the hangar. Bobby sat with Renee, fed her hunks of raw carrot, fondled her animatronic feet. Dietz was up on the wall in a handstand, babbling to Warren and the Rad Balm girl.

"Altamont? Best hologram I ever saw. Look, with the exception of Chuck Berry, every major entertainer was on a CIA payroll at one time or another. Doesn't matter much anymore. You kids, with your computers, your complacency beneath the boot of global capitalism, you've done in a few years what it took the pigs decades to put together."

"I'm an anarchist," said Warren.

"Let me tell you," said Dietz, "they're all immensely frightened."

"Well, what are you doing here then?" said the Rad Balm girl.

"Where was I supposed to go?"

I took a bench next to Desmond Mori, watched him spork kale from his bowl.

"I miss Parish's stew," I said.

"You knew the man they called Parish, then?"

"Why are you talking like that?"

"I'm sorry," said Desmond.

"What do you do here?"

"I'm the Chief Personal—"

"But what do you do?"

"I choose the chairs. I study ergonomics reports and choose the chairs. I respond to Frequently Asked Questions. I lead Team Greeting."

"It used to be called First Calling."

"Hey, don't tell me. I'm the only one who's even aware of shit like that around here. Except for the Pre-Realmers. Like Dietz and Renee. I always wanted to meet Heinrich. When I was a kid, a few years ago, I ordered his book through the mail. I guess he's not like he was, though."

"I wonder what happened to everybody," I said.

"Scattered."

"I like your vest."

"It's an exact replica of the one Naperson wore in the mothering hut."

"Naperton," I said.

"I was testing you," said Desmond.

Now Trubate's cackle burst across the hangar.

"Renee," he said, "you kill me. What are you even talking about? The Heinrich stuff is classic."

Dietz joined us on the bench, pointed over to Trubate and Renee.

"Look at them all cuddly together," he said. "Remember that old ad for the Poconos? They had those bathtubs shaped like pussies. Filled them with champagne."

"Hearts," I said.

"They put hearts in them?" said Dietz. "I thought it was champagne."

I waited for Renee to rise, tailed her to the serving table. Available now was some arid ziggurat of soy cakes and sunflower tortes.

"Dessert?" I said.

She pointed to the coffeepot and I drew her a cup of the house brew, yellow, sweet, carbonated, cold. Across the room Trubate was demonstrating the heroin walk he claimed to have perfected for a transgressive high-eight Hamlet.

"You've got to understand," I heard Trubate say, "the Prince of Denmark was a trust-fund brat."

"Well," I said to Renee, "as long as you love the guy."

"Love?"

Renee popped the top off a plastic vial, tapped out powder the texture of iron filings into her cup, sipped it.

"What's that for?" I said.

"I have a happiness-deficiency."

"Let's go," I said. "Let's get the hell out of here."

"You and me?" said Renee.

"Yeah."

"Steal the van?"

"Yeah."

"Hit the road?"

"That's it."

"Sleep under the stars with ketchup stains on our shirts?"

"Beautiful."

"You and me?"

"Screw Trubate," I said.

"I do," said Renee.

"What is it? Your chips? Your legs? We'll figure something out."

"No, we won't," said Renee. "Why do people always say that? We won't figure anything out. We'll stare at each other and wonder why the other person hasn't figured anything out. That fucker said we'd figure something out, and we haven't figured jack shit out. That's what we'll say to ourselves, and it's just a matter of time before we say it to each other."

Her head started to loll a little.

"You look really happy right now," I said.

Spit slid down her chin.

"Take me downstairs," she said. "I've got to do my miracle."

We rode an old cage elevator down to the lower levels. One of Desmond's reluctant acolytes rode the brake lever, whispered into his sleeve.

"Pathogens," I heard him say. "With a P."

"Aren't you supposed to be sick?" said Renee.

"Fine fettle," I said.

"You look pretty sick."

"That won't work," I said.

"Sure it will."

We hit bottom with a soft bump. The boy flipped the lever back.

"No," he was saying now, "you have to coat it before insertion. You didn't coat it, did you?"

We walked down a corridor and through a doorway into darkness. And then there was light, or lights, high blinding banks of them blasting down on an enormous soundstage. Camera crews clustered around a series of sets, three-walled ceilingless rooms, some white, some papered over with photo sheets of trees, or seascapes, or city squares at night. People scurried by with power strips and prop boxes. We passed the soil room, saw a masked man there in buckskin. He was tinier than he'd seemed on TV. He leaned on his shovel near a man spooling cable on his arm.

"Let's do one," said the man. He called for quiet and we stood off near some steel cases. The Digger dug, struck concrete, began his drag and scrape.

Renee led me away from the shovel screech.

"They'll shoot that shit for hours."

"What's the gimmick?" I said. "I don't get it. It's boring."

"We prefer trance-friendly."

Renee hobbled on towards the next set, a barren blue room with gym mats on the floor, a lone stool. Identical posters lined the wall. "Go, Gimp Snatch!" they said. The Rad Balm girl approached us with a clipboard.

"Sweetie," she said. "Feeling the magic?"

"I guess," said Renee.

"Hey, honey, you got a problem tonight?"

"No problem."

"Goody."

The Rad Balm girl smeared some ointment on her mouth.

"Where's the Spokesman?" said Renee.

"Warren? He's in makeup. I'll get him."

A few minutes later the kid with the muttonchops stepped bare-chested through the set door. He wore white, therapeutic-looking trousers, nurse shoes. He took a seat on the stool, started to knead his crotch.

"Places," said the Rad Balm girl.

Renee handed me her crutches, slid down to her belly at the lip of the stage.

"Action!"

Some song started pumping through the PA, the one I'd heard on the radio in Indiana, the authentic version, pre-viola. It sounded derivative now.

"I love my dog," Warren began, still fondling himself. "My dog loves me. That's all there is in life. I raised my dog from infancy. Puppyhood. Whatever. Both his parents were put down, so I had to do it myself. No help. Nobody gave a shit whether my dog lived or died. So I took it upon myself to give a shit. He was my dog. There are beautiful things in this world, and if you can escape your narcissism, or the collective hallucination of the media, or the singular hallucination of your narcissism, you might get to see them sometime. But it's like you're encased in some kind of fucking titanium pod cruising through the atmosphere, you're not quite the pilot but there's a joystick in your hand, and it feels like you're steering but you've never been steering, never in your life have you been steering, not when your dad remarried for the seventh time, not when your mom got weird and distant, not when your brother tried to butt in with the raising of your dog that you alone were raising from puppyhood, you've never been steering anything, really, you've just been cruising along in this pod with all these gleaming buttons on the control panel but they don't connect to anything, and you're just whistling along through the dead air, dead space, through the nothingness of the world's chatter and the nothingness of your own-most you jabbering away in your head, and you just have to get out of that pod, you must eject from the fucking pod, and you're like, Oh fuck, I must fucking eject, I must, I must fucking . . . and then you notice a little button that's gleaming, that's glowing a little differently from the others, and it's got a big E on it and it's glowing and it's even kind of like blinking as though maybe this button, as opposed to the other buttons, maybe this button actually fucking works, so you hit it, you hit it hard . . ."

Warren's cock popped out of his pants. Renee stabbed towards him on her elbows. Her legs swayed dead behind her. Occasionally, and with a terrible grunt, she'd put out her hand as though to grip air.

"Punching out," said Warren, his voice gaining velocity, "that's what they call ejection in all those jet pilot movies, where they're always going on about how you have to be careful punching out because you hit the wrong angle, boom, you lose an arm, you lose a head, you lose *your* head. But fuck it, I mean you can't go on in this pod, this little self-contained smugness apparatus of yours and—"

"Cut!" said the Rad Balm girl.

Renee collapsed near the tips of Warren's shoes, weeping.

"What?" said Warren.

"The dog," said the Rad Balm girl. "What happened to the dog?"

"I was looping back around to it."

"Renee was at her mark."

"I had a few seconds."

"Bullshit you did. Look at her. She's practically at your feet. Warren, this show isn't about you, it's about her. You have to be more generous."

"How is it about her? I'm the one talking. I'm the one beating off."

"That's the point. It's from a dyke's perspective."

I ducked out of there.

I wandered awhile, found a vault crammed with winking circuit boards, lay down and dozed on a hump of cable there. Maybe I dreamed. When I woke, somebody's boot tip nuzzling my ear, I did have that sense of being led out of some kind of subterrain, me discombobulated, a bit embarrassed, a tourist nearly lost in some regionally famous cave.

It was Desmond's boot. I studied the palisades of grain in the leather.

"He's up now. He'd like to see you."

Desmond walked me out to my mark, took my arm as I went to open the thin pine door.

"Just be yourself," he said.

"Just let go of my arm."

Heinrich sat up in his hospital bed, tissue balls and clementine peels spilled out on the counterpane. The sky on the wallpaper was paler than I'd seen on TV, the desert darker.

"Steve-o!" called the studio audience. You could hear the tape hiss as the cries died down to some stray handclaps, a few knowing hoots.

Steve-o devotees.

"Do my tumors understand that when I go, they go, too?" said Heinrich.

I looked around for cue cards. Spotlights popped.

"Tumors," I said. "Tumors shmoomers."

"Cut!"

Trubate bobbed up out of the darkness.

"What the fuck was that?"

"Ad lib," I said.

"Ad lib," said Trubate.

"That's right."

"Listen," said Trubate, "don't wait for the laugh track. Makes you look like an amateur."

"I am an amateur."

"Point taken. Just don't ruin my show."

"Or what?"

"I'm a sick man," said Trubate. "And I don't have the luxury of dying, like you do. I have to live with my sickness. I have to take it out on other people. Or the people other people care about."

"Is that a threat?"

"Vague. Veiled."

He stuck an old light meter under my chin. The dial

didn't move, looked busted, and Trubate didn't check it anyway.

"Let's take it from the dead dad speech," he said.

Heinrich coughed, pulled a clementine from a sack that hung on his bedpost, started to peel it down.

"You know," he said, "I watched my old man die. Kind of like this. He gathered us all to him. He said he had something to show us. When we were all there in the room he lifted up his blanket, pointed down to his bedpan. To what was in the bedpan. 'There it is,' he said. 'I wish I could leave you more.' He was dead by dusk."

"I don't believe that story," I said.

"Jeez, you want a gazelle?"

He had his tongue out. It was hard to tell if he was razzing me, or just gagging, dry.

"Can I get you some water?"

His eyelids were caked with paste. Beige fluid frothed at the hems of his mouth. He shuddered like some piece of overheating machinery.

"Hey," called Trubate from the darkness, "Code Blue Man!"

The Philosopher leaped through the door in his Lycra hood, a heel of French bread in his hand. The recorded applause was a concert-hall roar, maybe something bootlegged from a diva's farewell. The Philosopher did some bug-eyed business to the camera, a vampy strut to the bed. He sopped up Heinrich's froth with his baguette.

"Won't be long now," he said. "Vitals are locking down. Big choo-choo's comin' round the bend. All aboard!"

"This is a man here," I said. "A man dying. Have some respect."

Heinrich made more noises. Froth fluttered up.

"Meat, meat, meat," said the Philosopher. "You, too, pal."

"I'm in fine fettle," I said.

"That's how you're supposed to feel in the final stages of PREXIS. Haven't you heard the news? How I discovered virulent Goldfarb clusters within the original PREXIS protein model?"

"PREXIS schmexis," I said.

Laughter boomed out of the walls.

The Philosopher fell on me. We pitched down to concrete. I kicked, caught him with my knee, flew at him with both fists, windmilling. Rain of blows. Steady rain of blows. My knuckle came up with a piece of blue-stained tooth.

Now Heinrich started to stir, thrash, blow froth, a sea beast sounding. I went to him, took his hand.

"Herodotus," he whispered, "writes of an army that went away to war for twenty-eight years. When they returned home they found themselves locked out of their city. Their wives, you see, had married their slaves. A new generation had grown up and seized power. The last thing these slave sons wanted was the masters of their fathers back in town. Day after day the old army stormed the city. Day after day the slave sons drove them back. At last one of the wizened old generals said, 'If we keep attacking them with swords and spears they will consider themselves our equals and they will keep beating us back. We must go to them with whips.' And so they did. And when the slave sons saw the masters of their fathers come to the city walls with whips, they fled."

Heinrich's hand drooped down along the bed skirt. I thought it a sign, some finality of musculature, a swoop deathward. But he was just strumming the fabric down there with his thumb. Boredom, itch, even now.

"I genuinely prefer tangerines," he said, turned to the wall dunes, died.

"Cut!" called Trubate from the darkness. "That was dynamite."

Someone scurried up to cover Heinrich with a sheet. The Philosopher was kneeling on the floor, feeling around for his teeth.

"Goldfarb what?" I said to him.

"Cluthterth," he said through his ruined mouth.

"I believe you."

"Fuf nath ta beleef?"

The Digger and I dug the hole at daybreak. We dug it near the rockpile behind the hangar. The clouds were the color of our shovel blades. The Digger looked to be suffering under his ski mask.

"Why don't you take that thing off?" I said.

He stared at me through slits in the wool.

The rest of them stood in a ring around us. Trubate, Desmond, Warren, Dietz, all the Realmers, dozens of them, most dozing in the heat. The Philosopher sat a little ways off, his mouth stuffed with gauze.

They'd carried Heinrich out on a battered boogie board, shrouded him in counterpane. A pair of mint-condition quarter pieces commemorating the statehood of New Jersey rested on his eyelids.

"Coins of a darker realm," said Desmond.

They slid Heinrich into the hole.

"That's it?" said Renee.

"What else is there?" said Trubate.

"When my dog died," said Warren, "we buried him just like this. And we all threw something in that reminded us of him. Dog toys, dog biscuits, essays in which I'd mentioned my dog."

"That's so beautiful," said the Rad Balm girl.

"Oh, is it?" said Renee. "Why don't we just throw you in."

"Go ahead," said the Rad Balm girl. "See if you can find another technologist who'll work for stock options these days."

"Cunt," said Renee.

"Silly cunt," called one of the New Zealanders.

I started to walk away.

"Where are you going, Steve?" said Trubate.

"I'm leaving."

"You can't leave. Don't you get that? Damn, you of all people."

I walked off in the direction I'd come with Dietz. Somewhere up ahead was the abandoned campsite. Past that was the runway. I could wait for the plane. Maybe the plane was due back. Doubtful, but possible. What wasn't possible?

I'd gone in for a checkup.

I could hear Trubate shouting down his people behind me. I kept walking, walking through the pain, walking it off, moving through my moist crackle and burst. I pictured each step shucking those Goldfarb clusters loose, little protein deathsquads bouncing along in miniature humvees through the bleak ravines of me. They had names like Reynoldo, Spider, Wideband, wore paramilitary underwear manufactured in

Rhode Island. Ever since the Philosopher had told me about the clusters I'd been feeling them on the move. Psychosomatic? Later, towards the end, I asked him.

"Psychosomatic like a heart attack," he said.

Now Dietz caught up with me.

"What are you doing?" he said.

"What do you mean?"

"He'll shoot you."

"Paranoid hippie fuck," I said.

I heard the crack, the whistle, felt the punch in my spine.

Items #9

FAQ #3:
Why does Steve deny his name is Steve?

He hated his name. There was nothing to his name. There
was taunt built into it because of its nothingness. It sounded
like something you wiped off your shirt. Everyone was supposed to be special but how could you be special if your name
was tantamount to lint? He stayed in his room and read
books. He stayed in his room and read the beginnings of
books, until there was mention of a breast heaving, or a groin

tightening. Then he'd put the book aside for a few minutes. He could do it over and over again, for hours. He'd skip school to do it.

He knew what was special.

His mother said he was too shy. His only friend was Cudahy. They used to burn trees. Sometimes he'd sit by himself in his father's toolshed, study the lawn mower blade in his lap. He'd run his thumb over the rust, up to the toothy crack near the tip. Something might scuttle in the rake bin behind him. Field mice, his father called them. Field mice ran free in the fields. They had freedoms we couldn't dream.

They had no names.

What he'd seen his father do with Cudahy's father, there was a name for that. That wasn't anything, though. Kids did stuff like that all the time. It was weird, was all, like seeing your old man on a moped.

He got more Steve years on him. It was time to be in the world. The world was like God or some fucked-up dragon. You couldn't look at it all at once or you'd go nuts.

He fell in with a woman who believed in falling in love. They made a creature together. People made creatures to pass themselves onward, but that's not how he saw it. He wanted to stop the Steveness. He needed a family to destroy him, his Steveness. Someday he'd make a new name for himself. Before he died he'd have a new name, or no name.

It wouldn't be the name his mother used to call him when she called him in for dinner from the stoop.

"Stee-eeve!" she used to call.

Once, his buddy Cudahy grinned.

"Tell her fuck you."

They'd been wrestling in the grass. Greco-Roman. American. Fake American.

"Fuck you, Mom!" he called across the yard.

He had to eat dinner on his bed. The penalty for insolence is room service. He couldn't eat, though. He couldn't get it down. It was because of the guilt. He said it was because of the broccoli.

FAQ #7
What does Steve eat?

He eats what's brought to him. Water, bread and water, sometimes stew. The Realms community decides his dinner daily. Steve has joked that he can gauge the mood of the nation by the size of his portion. Some days the nation is in a generous mood. Some days, maybe, the generous majority is busy. Those days the people Steve tends to call the bastards log on to the Subject Steve. Just Water, they shout at their screens. Of course, there are those who have already visited **The Tool Shed** and downloaded the latest **thought command** application. They don't have to say anything at all!

They just think just water, and just water it is!

FAQ #9
When is Steve not available for viewing?

Never is Steve not available for viewing. There are cameras **on** him all the time. There are cameras **in** him all the time.

FAQ #14
Is the Subject Steve a game?

The Subject Steve (TM) is a revolutionary media space that binds together the most innovative elements of gaming, spectacle, democracy, and commerce. It is produced by **The Realms** in association with the **Goldfarb-Blackstone Life Lab.**

FAQ #15
What is the significance of the mothering hut?

The hut Steve inhabits, housed in the main facility, is an exact replica of the one erected by the late Heinrich of Newark at the now-defunct Center for Nondenominational Recovery and Redemption. It was used for purification purposes and to hasten personal growth. The Realms, as many know, is indebted to the teachings of Heinrich, but its methods and goals must be situated in a much larger context. **Read** Realms-founder Robertson Trubate's mission statement for more information.

FAQ #17
How long does Steve have to live?

It's difficult to calculate. By our calculations there can be no calculations. He is dying of something no one has ever died of before. He is dying of something absolutely, fantastically new. Click here for his medical **chart** or visit the Realms **archives** for a peek at the top-secret notes Goldfarb and Blackstone took during those first, exciting consultations. Click here for a **dimensional model** of the deadly Goldfarb protein.

FAQ #22
Is Steve's item book posted in its entirety?

It will never be complete until Steve himself achieves ultimate completion.

FAQ #25
Does Steve deserve our sympathy?

We'll let the Realmers speak to that. Here's a transcript from comments made earlier this week in the Special Cases Lounge, one of our most popular rooms.

> **gary7:** fuck steve . . . anybody here?
> **burma:** steve O fuck that fucker die already!
> **nonabravo:** he's misunderstood
> **burma:** this twaddle again? i say fuck steve
> **gary7:** bad dad bad hubby.
> **nonabravo:** less than bad. worse.
> **reneelegs:** He thinks he made me come.
> **bundiscakes:** Sad Less than sad.
> **gary7:** fuck him
> **machinaX:** right on baby!
> **nonabravo:** did you see that bio on his father?
> **seawolf:** inner monsoon my ass.
> **steve:** Hey, it's me.

gary7: fuck you get the fuck out of here.

reneelegs: steve you should go.

burma: you're ruining it dude.

gary7: go the fuck you fuck.

"You're a hit," said Bobby Trubate. "But watch it with all the scribbling. Better you babble than scribble. Better yet, moan. Steve, they love the moans. They love the mealtimes. They dig dialogue, conversations, say. The conversation we're having now? They love it. We have data. Your pathetic attempts at masturbation? The rubbing? They adore this. Hell, they even tune in for your naps. But the writing, I mean, have you ever watched somebody write? What are you fooling around with that stupid item book for, anyway? The rest of us burned ours, you know. After we buried Heinrich. Very ritualistic. Very moving."

"I'm not done with mine."

"Well, I'm not going to stop you. More Steve content. For later. Do you know what I mean when I say for later?"

"Yes," I said.

"The bed restraints aren't too tight, are they?"

"No, they're great."

"Do you have enough arm motion?"

"Sure."

"How's your back?"

"I don't know. I'm restrained."

"I'm sure it's fine," said Trubate. "I'm sorry I shot you. But I bet you're pretty stoked it was a rubber bullet. I ordered them by mistake, but then I figured, rubber gets the job done. I'm not here to kill people."

"No, I suppose not."

"I mean Heinrich would have killed your ass. Bailing on his funeral like that."

"I guess so."

"I'm on your side. Not that there are sides, but if there were sides, I'd consider myself on your side."

"Thanks."

"Steve, do you know that I love you?"

"I didn't know that," I said.

"Now you know. I was going to say, not in a sexual way, but what the hell does that mean? I love you in every way. We're all post-human here, right? I'm not afraid. Are you afraid?"

He pointed to a canvas satchel on the wall, Heinrich's old pain kit.

Branks, breast-ripper, pear.

He looked up into one of the cameras in the thatch.

"Realmers," he said, "are you ready for more show!?"

The Philosopher came by for a visit.

"You," I said.

"Me," he said, bared his new blazing teeth.

"Nice," I said.

"Had to fly up north for them," said the Philosopher. "Find a mouth guy Blackstone hadn't turned against me."

"The Mechanic," I said.

"We're in heavy litigation."

"Sorry to hear it."

"Don't be," said the Philosopher. "I consider it a continuation of our collaboration by other means."

He smoothed his hand on his hood.

"Why do you wear that?" I said.

"I'm Code Blue Man."

"Like a superhero?"

"People are frightened by science. This makes them feel more comfortable. Are you comfortable?"

He lifted a long syringe from a felt-lined case.

"What's that?"

"It's just a prop. People want more injections."

"There's stuff in it."

"Yes, there's stuff in it."

"What's the stuff?"

"Prop stuff. Now, if you'll allow me to lift your gown for a moment."

"Why?"

"Because," said the Philosopher, his voice loud for the microphones, "I need to take this frighteningly large needle and inject the sensitive tip of your penis!"

"No!" I said.

"It's crucial to your treatment!" he shouted.

"Please," I said.

"Just trust me," he said.

I decided to trust him. I figured he meant to fake it. I could sense a weariness in him, some seismic disgust with the entire enterprise.

I guess I figured wrong.

Time went by, probably. It was hard to keep track. The Realms launched a news division, a twenty-four-hour, continuously updated wire service, but the news was always at least several hundred years old. "False Messiah Leads Jews Awry in Smyrna," read one headline. "Pre-Classic Mayan Ritual to Include Hallucinogenic Enema," went another. Maybe it was all part of continuum awareness training.

Maybe it was all part of a plan.

Didn't it all have to be part of a plan?

The Rad Balm girl said it could well be.

The Rad Balm girl said there were big plans for my finale, too.

"My finale?" I said.

"We're days away," she said. "Bobby's given us the green light. Traffic is slowing down so it's time for the green light. The green light is going to be the light at the end of the tunnel. But it might not be green. It will be Heavenly, which I think of as white. But those are my prejudices speaking. My prejudices speak me. But sometimes they're right on the money."

"You're confusing me."

"I'm crystal on this. The Subject Steve must reach a satisfactory conclusion. A conclusion of total satisfaction-saturation. For all parties concerned. I need you to sign this waiver."

She handed me some stapled pages, a Bic ballpoint.

"Read it after you sign it," she said. "You know you're going to sign it anyway. You don't have to feign scrutiny. It's crucial that we stay crystal now."

I signed the waiver, the warrant, whatever it was.

I started to murmur so the Rad Balm girl would lean down.

I stabbed her in the neck with the Bic.

. . .

The Digger appeared in the doorway of the hut. I'd noticed him staring in from time to time, wordless, eyes flashing from behind his ski mask, but he'd never been so brazen before. Now he walked into the room and stood near an oil portrait of Heinrich painted on black velvet. It hung from a hook in the thatch. *Soldier, Healer, Dreamer* said the brass plate.

"How is she?" I said.

He looked away for a while, as though wondering if he should speak.

"She'll live," he said.

"Why don't you take your mask off? I know you, don't I? Where do I know you from?"

"I need to tell you," he said. "I've been asked to dig you a hole."

"Will I be dead when they put me in it?"

"That's an interesting question."

"Will you answer it?"

"I wish I would," said the Digger.

Desmond rolled in some covered dishes on a cart.

"Sure it's safe?" I said. "I'm a psycho now."

"I'll take my chances. Anyway, they're watching us. The whole world is watching us. This is your last meal."

"Don't I get to choose?"

My last bacon cheeseburger was a bit too bacony.

"How is it?" said Desmond.

"Delicious."

"We polled the Realms. Baked Alaska got nipped at the wire. Can I have a bite?"

I tore some burger off for Desmond.

"Damn," he said. "This is the shit. All that clean Asian food around here makes me sick. You know, my father was a flavor engineer."

"I didn't know that."

"God, I remember all the crazy guys that worked at his lab. Did stuff just for a goof. One guy, he made this steak sauce. He called it Holocaust-flavored. He bottled the shit and he—"

"I think I'd like to be alone now."

"I understand. But do you mind if I ask you one question?"

"One question," I said.

"How did you go on living knowing you were going to die?"

"Was I living?" I said.

"Wow," said Desmond. "Don't talk. Don't say another thing. Those should be your last words. Mythic, man. I knew you had style."

"Fuck you," I said.

"See, you ruined it. You always ruin it, don't you?"

"We said one question," I said.

Desmond stood and raised his hand towards the wall thatch. A woman in a mink brassiere walked into the room. Fair Dinkum.

"This is Tina," said Desmond, shut the door behind him.

Tina took a seat near my bed.

"I like your tattoo," I said. "Is that a water bottle?"

"Look," she said. "I'm not attracted to you in any way, but I'm supposed to offer you some kind of final sexual favor in the way of sex and stuff. Nobody else wanted to, so, of course, I'm like, I volunteer. I'm the little trooper, aren't I? Mom? Mom? Can you hear me, Mom? She's not dead, but it's like she's hovering all the time anyway. She's like, Tina, if everybody was like I'm not jumping off the bridge, and so on. Oh, well. So, what do you think? A little hoobie doobie? Some jobby wobby?"

"Jobby wobby," I said.

"Did I say jobby wobby? I didn't mean jobby wobby. I could shit on your cock, though."

She plucked at her lip stud.

They wheeled me out to the desert in my bed. They wheeled me out across the scrub, took me up to a little hillock of hard earth. They maybe meant to murder me with sunlight. Baked Steve. Devil's Steve Cake. Old Gold and the Rad Balm girl rigged lights and video gear. Dietz squatted by my gurney, rubbed my skull.

"I'll see you on the other side, bro," he said. "Or if there's no other side, then, well, I guess I'm seeing you right now."

Trubate was sweat-resplendent in his robe. He paced about his minions, muttered something about turning water into vitamin water, hummed. It was the aardvark song. I must have hummed it in my sleep. Maybe the nation was humming it by now.

"Fiona," I said.

The Digger was nearly done with the hole. The task had maybe taken a toll on him. He fell to his knees in the dirt, let some air in under his mask. I saw an odd lump of skin there.

"We're good to go," said the Rad Balm girl.

"Fucking finally," said Bobby. "Where's Warren? Don't we get another doggie speech?"

"Warren's not coming," said the Rad Balm girl. "He says his presence would send the wrong message to his readers."

"Pussy," said Trubate. "Pussy readers."

The Rad Balm girl held me down, saw me notice the bandage on her throat, dug her thumbnail into my ear. Old Gold unbuckled my bed straps, bound me up with rope. He ripped my gown away, picked up a tray of cold grease. I could make out shreds of last night's chuck, my mythic bacon cheese. Old Gold scooped up handfuls of the stuff, smeared me down like a channel swimmer. Sunlight was too easy. They meant to bait the beasts out of the desert night, the ants and wolves and wolverines, the carrion-loving birds, all of God's meat-horny Steve-craving things.

Renee stood off and watched, crutch tips sinking in sand.

"They could have voted for something much crueler," Trubate kept saying. "You should be thankful. Grateful. Thankful."

The Philosopher stood over me with his new marvelous mouth.

"I want you to know that in all my years of science I've never come across a subject as worthy of the name as you. I'll tell them what you did here this day. At cocktail parties. At informal seminars. Do you have anything to say before the ball gag goes in?"

"Excuse me?"

"Eighty-three percent of respondents weighed in for the gag option. Seventy-four percent of those people, incidentally, also regularly purchase home decor products online. Don't know what it means, really, but the people of the Realms have spoken. Do you have anything to say to the world?"

"I'm thirsty."

"That's it?"

"The Realms is not the Realms!" I said.

"Anything else?"

"It's all hype! You're being duped! The goose has no clothes! The president is a moon rock! Eden is a fuck club!"

"Take your time."

"The server is not secure!"

"Gag him!"

The Rad Balm girl rammed the ball in my mouth, cinched it tight. Old Gold tipped me into the hole. I kept squinching my eyes, waiting for dirt to splash down, but then I remembered the cameras, the burger fat. The Digger stood staring from the lip of the hole. It would have made for a menacing shot. Maybe it did. My ball gag probably had a camera, too. The Digger leaned down and tugged his ski mask off his head. He had a nylon stocking on beneath it.

FAQ #23
How fucked is the Subject Steve?

Hard to say. One could argue, for instance, that fuckedness is a vague concept, indefinable, and thus a meaningless point of departure for any sort of cogent analysis. Yet by the same token, one could make room for the advent of a counterargument, whereby fuckedness is posited as something else entirely. Feel free to **voice** your opinion.

I shivered in my pit, stared up at the stars. There were forms now finally in these decals of the void, I could see it, a cosmos of my own, a god grid tailored to this niche of one. Up in the bitter firmament Cudahy heaved his shot and Fiona picked her pock and a box of Hinks Civic stainless nibs spilled out in milky light. Here was Renee, frozen in her sneeze of sorrow, and Captain Thornfield's captainless hat. There was Heinrich preaching from his porch, Bobby in his blazing robe, Estelle in lewd galactic concourse with her only spawn, big jiz splooging across the vaults of heaven. There was Donald, his stars stifled somehow, and the Kincaids, Big Fran and Little Fran, indistinguishable save for the far stars that looped to make the apron string bow. Here was William, young William, with his straw of happiness, his art rock toupee. Here was Maryse asquat a chamber pot filled with candied yams, a viscid bile coursing down her chin. There was my mother, the navigator, flying through the star shatter of some celestial head-on, a Ziploc bag of Cheez-Its in her fist. I saw them all up there, the Philosopher and the Mechanic, two-faced, one-hooded, a fire-sale Janus, Greta and Clarice double-dipping Jesus, Mr. Ferguson, Wendell Tarr, Dr. Cornwallis, the Rad Balm girl. There were even bears up there. I saw fucking bears up there. But where was Steve? I searched the suns of night for a constellated me.

FAQ #27
What the hell ever happened to Steve?

The Subject Steve is without a doubt a dead subject. He's probably dead in the desert somewhere, though initial air searches have recovered nothing but a stolen van and a diary. We surmise Steve ran out of gas and staggered off into the waste.

Whether his disease or the elements claimed him first we will never know. Click here to **cook up** a theory, or click here to **order** souvenirs from Steve's life, including his Jews of Jazz calendar and snapshots of his family. Click here for spycam video of his sexy daughter in **flagrante delicioso**! Click here for a **peek** at the newest offerings from the Realms, *Inside the Mothering Hut* and *It's Your Funeral: The Digger DaShawn Digs Real-Life Graves*.

I heard footsteps, too quick for people feet. They had the pouncy sound of people-hunters. I heard barks and breathing. Dogs, desert dogs. Hell's hounds here for their treat. I looked up from my hole, saw cold eyes burn green in fur.

Let the bastards note, I thought.

"Fuhk Oo," I said into my ball gag.

"Hey," said a voice, "don't talk to my dog that way."

Warren vaulted down into the hole. He had a steak knife in his hand. His wolfhound hopped in after him, sniffed my hair.

"No, Pascal," said Warren, shinned the dog off, cut my ropes.

I tried to get up, fell back in the hole.

"Here," said Warren, hoisted me out.

Far off I could see the lights of the hangar. The redemption van rumbled towards us with the headlights dimmed.

"I thought your dog was dead," I said.

"I'm an artist," said Warren.

"Why are you doing this?"

"I don't know. I guess I'm just tired of the bullshit."

"What bullshit?"

"I don't know."

"You're the spokesman of your generation."

"Yeah."

"You're not really articulating."

"Steve, I'm saving your life."

"Thanks."

"Look," said Warren, "someday my name will come up in conversation, as it seems to so goddamn often these days. Some of your friends will scoff at my work, all the attention it's been paid. Hype, they'll say. Marketing. A dearth of authentic talent. But you'll stick up for me. You guys don't know what the hell you're talking about, you'll say. That guy saved my fucking life."

I wanted to tell him I'd be dead by then, that maybe he should talk to Spider or Wideband about this.

Now the van rolled up and Trubate was out the door. He wiped at his nose with his robe sleeve.

"Fucking outstanding," he said. "Fucking beautiful. A rescue mission. Now I know why I went through all that bullshit with your jerk lawyers, Warren. You are a motherfucking genius. You are without a doubt the most significant artist of your generation. Now where do you want it?"

Trubate got his gun out. Warren whipped the knife. The blade wheeled in high-watt light. The grip hit Trubate in the eye. He drew his hands up to cup it, hollered, staggered back, let the gun drop. I dove on the thing, stood slowly with a bead on Trubate.

"You don't have the balls to shoot me," he said.

He squirmed in the sand. Fluid from his eye squirted down his cheek.

"I never did," I said. "I never had the balls for anything, Bobby. I'm a ball-less wonder. De-balled. Sans balls. Without balls."

"That's all I meant," said Trubate.

I shot him in the head.

"Shit," he moaned.

Warren went over to where Trubate lay.

"No blood."

"Rubber bullet," I said.

"I think you stunned him," said Warren.

"I'm stunned," said Trubate. "I don't fucking believe this."

"Fuf nath ta beleef?" I said.

"What did he say?" said Trubate. "What did that mother-fucker say?"

"Slap leather," I said. "Fill your hand."

"You'd better go," said Warren.

"Need a ride?"

"I'd better stay. I'm under contract."

"Me, too, I guess."

"Not for what I'm getting."

"You're a good man," I said.

"I don't know about that," said Warren. "I feel more like a boy. Everybody my age does. It's like we're all trying to come to terms with a moment that won't quite reveal itself, and here we are, devoid of a context within which to situate our-selves—"

"Warren," I said.

"What?"

I got in the van, drove out across the desert floor. The desert was forever. The whole wide world was a road. There were lit shapes in the distance. Hills, houses, power lines, who knew?

The van shook as it picked up speed. The steering wheel stabbed my hands. The radio was full of static. I could have sworn I heard a voice there just the same.

It said, This ain't no joke, Jack.

It said, Fare thee well.

Many thanks to Gerry Howard for his wisdom and skill and to Ira Silverberg for his faith and diligence. Thanks to my family and friends and friends of the family. Thanks to Gordon Lish. Thanks to the Supreme Council of the Squanderers—Alex Abramovich, John Barr, Lucas Hendrich, Tom Moore—and to Marc Maron, co-drafter of the Astoria Statement.

The author also wishes to thank the subject.

CRITICALLY ACCLAIMED FICTION
BY SAM LIPSYTE

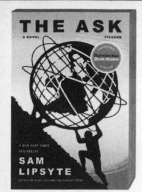

THE ASK
A Novel

A *New York Times Book Review* Notable Book of the Year

"A great comic novel." —*GQ*

ISBN 978-0-312-68063-3 (Paperback)
$15.00/$17.00 Can.

THE SUBJECT STEVE
A Novel

"In a time when the language of most novels
is dead on arrival, this book, about a dying man,
is startlingly alive." —JEFFREY EUGENIDES

ISBN 978-0-312-42997-3 (Paperback)
$14.00/$16.00 Can.

VENUS DRIVE
Stories

"These are torqued-up, enthusiastically black-hearted stories
by a grimly cheerful author." —PADGETT POWELL

ISBN 978-0-312-42960-7 (Paperback)
$14.00/$17.00 Can.

HOME LAND
A Novel

"Genius. As eloquent and delirious a rant I've heard since
Henry Miller was doing the ranting." —GARY SHTEYNGART

ISBN 978-0-312-42418-3 (Paperback)
$15.00/$18.00 Can.

PICADOR
www.picadorusa.com

Available wherever books are sold, or call 1-800-330-8477 to order.